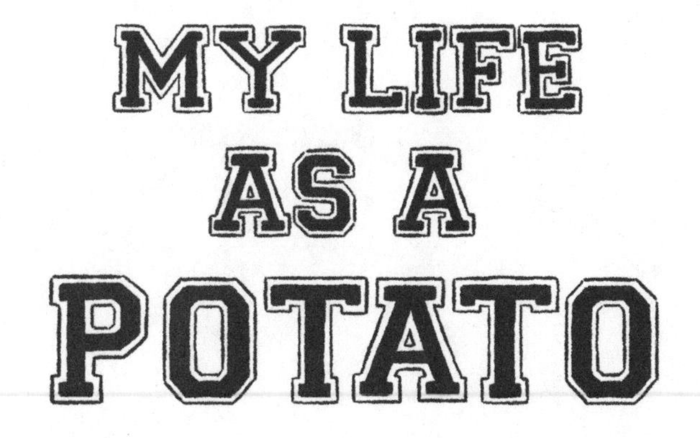
MY LIFE
AS A
POTATO

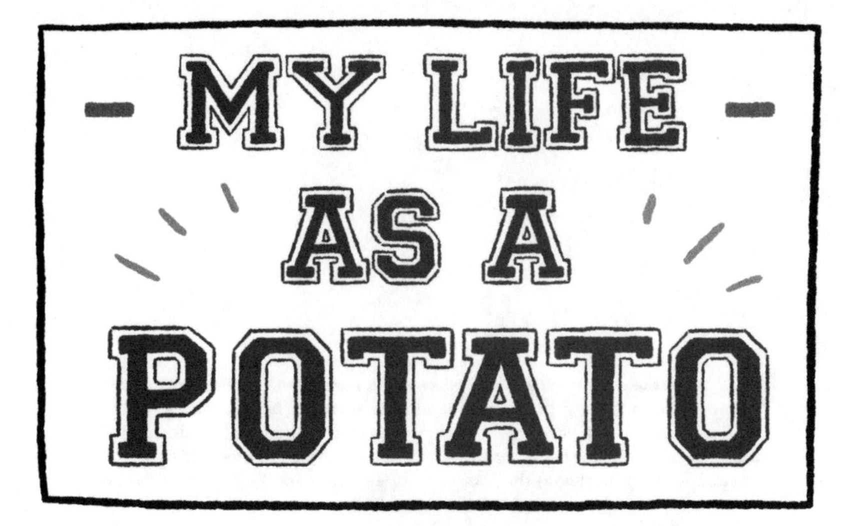

BY
ARIANNE COSTNER

ILLUSTRATED BY
JAMES LANCETT

Random House New York

This is a work of fiction. All incidents and dialogue, and all characters
with the exception of some well-known historical and public figures,
are products of the author's imagination and are not to be construed as real.
Where real-life historical or public figures appear, the situations, incidents, and
dialogues concerning those persons are fictional and are not intended to depict
actual events or to change the fictional nature of the work. In all other respects,
any resemblance to persons living or dead is entirely coincidental.

 Published in the United States by Random House Children's Books,
a division of Penguin Random House LLC, New York.

Random House and the colophon are registered trademarks of
Penguin Random House LLC.

Visit us on the Web! rhcbooks.com

Educators and librarians, for a variety of teaching tools,
visit us at RHTeachersLibrarians.com

Library of Congress Cataloging-in-Publication Data
Names: Costner, Arianne, author. | Lancett, James, illustrator.
Title: My life as a potato / Arianne Costner; illustrated by James Lancett.
Description: First edition. | New York: Random House, [2020] |
Summary: "When Ben Hardy is forced to become the school's mascot,
Steve the Spud, he wants to keep the embarrassing gig a secret
at all costs."—Provided by publisher.
Identifiers: LCCN 2019000239 | ISBN 978-0-593-11866-5 (hardcover) |
ISBN 978-0-593-11867-2 (lib. bdg.) | ISBN 978-0-593-11868-9 (ebook)
Subjects: | CYAC: Mascots—Fiction. | Potatoes—Fiction. |
Middle schools—Fiction. | Schools—Fiction. | Humorous stories.
Classification: LCC PZ7.1.C6747 My 2020 | DDC [Fic]—dc23

Printed in the United States of America
10 9 8 7 6 5 4 3
First Edition

Random House Children's Books supports the First Amendment
and celebrates the right to read.

For my children, the joys of my life

—AC

For my amazing wife, Marta—

my best friend and biggest inspiration

—JL

MY LIFE
AS A
POTATO

1

The Curse of the Potato

I don't know what I did to deserve it, but the fact is clear: I, Ben Hardy, am cursed by potatoes. That demon veggie has been out to get me for years.

Evidence #1: When I was five, I tripped over a bag of potatoes and broke my arm. I had to wear an itchy green cast for six weeks.

Evidence #2: My mom makes the world's gluey-est mashed potatoes. They're great for craft projects. Not for eating.

Evidence #3: There's a faded scar above my left eyebrow. What happened? Let's just say I got on the bad side of a cat named Tater Tot.

Then, two weeks ago, right in the middle of seventh grade, my family moved from Los Angeles to South Fork, Idaho—aka "the Potato Capital of the World." The people here worship the veggie like my dad worships the Lakers.

Case in point: my new school's game-day shirt. Today about half the school showed up wearing one. When I reach the cafeteria for lunch, I realize my friend Ellie is part of that half.

"You have to get one, Ben. Where's your school spirit?" Ellie plunks her lunch tray down and tosses her long black braid over her shoulder. On her shirt, a cartoon potato flexes its bulky biceps and flashes the kind of smile that should be reserved for clowns in horror movies.

Out of all the mascot options—the Cougars, the Eagles, the Saber-Toothed Tigers—my new school just *had* to be the Spuds. This crosses a line. At my last school, we were the Wildcats, ferocious and intimidating. All a potato can scare is . . . well, me, I guess.

I shake my head. "No way am I spending twenty bucks on that shirt. I could buy ten extra-large Slurpees for that price."

"What about Slurpees?" Our friend Hunter pulls off his hoodie as he sits at our table. He's wearing the shirt too. Somehow these two are totally oblivious to the uncoolness of waltzing around with a potato on your chest.

Ellie looks at Hunter. "No Slurpees. I'm just trying to get Ben to buy the game-day shirt. You're going with us tonight, right?"

"Can't," he says. "I'm still on foal watch." Hunter's horse Misty is super pregnant, so he and his dad have to sleep outside her stable in case she goes into labor. This is the kind of stuff people do in South Fork, Idaho.

Moving to a small town has been, to use Mom's words, "a bit of a culture shock." On the bright side, South Fork has less traffic and less smog. But then, there's no beach. No In-N-Out Burger. No skate park. On my first day, I showed up to school with a new haircut that would've been totally normal back in LA—short on the sides and swoopy on top. Too bad no one here has that haircut. I might as well have dyed my hair purple, I stick out so much.

Ellie shrugs at me. "Guess it's just us tonight. At least wear red."

I chug the rest of my chocolate milk. "Deal." Here's the best part about Idaho: Hunter and Ellie. Back in California, I didn't have anyone I could just go to basketball games with. My best friend moved to Canada at the beginning of the school year, so I ended up with a handful of sorta friends, but not a lot of hang-out friends. Sorta friends are the people you talk with about homework or mean teachers. Hang-out friends are the people you share food with or walk home with after school.

Hunter and I became friends when he offered me some Cheetos in science class on my first day. I helped him with his worksheet in return. The next day, he invited me to sit with him and Ellie in the cafeteria, which I appreciated, since, let's face it, the worst part of being the new kid is wondering who you'll eat with at lunch.

Sitting with Hunter and Ellie felt comfortable, like switching into sweatpants after school. They're the kind of people you can crack up with over dumb stuff, like Hunter's horrible Chewbacca impression or pictures of Ellie's poodle wearing socks. Last week, Ellie and I realized we live on the same street, so we've started walking home together. It makes trudging through the January weather a lot more bearable.

"Agh!" Hunter peers into his lunch sack, and his eyes bug out of his head. "Look what my mom packed me. A Go-Gurt and a can of tuna! With a can opener and everything! I can't eat this in public!"

"Then learn to make your own lunch," Ellie says.

"Learn to make your own face," says Hunter.

"That doesn't even make sense," says Ellie. She holds out half a sandwich. "Here, take this. I don't really like avocado anyway."

"What?" Hunter's face falls. "How can you not like avocado?"

She wrinkles her nose. "I think it's the texture."

"But . . . guacamole!"

"Just accept the sandwich!"

I try to stay out of these Ellie-and-Hunter arguments. They bicker like two people who've been stuck in the back seat of a car for nine hours. At first I thought it was because they were flirting, but—plot twist—they're just cousins. It's not obvious they're related. Hunter takes after the blue-eyed, pale-skinned white side of the family. Ellie has her Latina mom's brown eyes and complexion. If you look close enough, though, you'll notice the matching freckles across their noses.

I'm about to offer Hunter my string cheese when he jumps out of his seat and points under the table next to us. "Hot dog!"

Ellie buries her face in her hands. "Not again."

Hunter's obsessed with Chuck the Hot Dog, a game that's been popular at South Fork Middle School since the beginning of time, apparently. The cafeteria hot dogs are so rubbery that no one wants to eat them. They're more like pink erasers than meat. You can usually find them lying under tables or kicked into corners. Naturally, a game has sprung up where people throw them to see who can get the most bounces. (When no teachers are watching, of course.) Legend has it someone got twelve bounces once. Hunter says he's never gotten more than three or four.

Hunter ducks under the bench and crawls through a mob of knees. There's no time for dignity when a hot dog is involved. A minute later he reemerges, hot dog in hand. His proud face reminds me of the one Buster—my corgi—makes when we play fetch. They even have the same shaggy blond hair.

"Your turn." Hunter places the hot dog in my hand, and it's perfect. No squishes. No tears. Everything needed for optimum bounce-age.

But I don't want detention. Last week, Hunter got his "final warning" from the cafeteria monitor. Since we're friends, this "final warning" probably extends to me. I scan the room, fully expecting to see the monitor marching toward us with her stern expression. Luckily, it looks like she stepped out of the room.

"Hey, Ben's gonna chuck the hot dog!" A basketball player from two tables over points at me, and his teammates cheer me on. I had no idea that guy knew my name.

"You do it." I shove the hot dog back at Hunter, but he dodges.

"No, dude, you. It's his turn, right, Ellie?"

She lifts her palms up. "Leave me out of it. I'd rather you chuck it in the trash."

The basketball table stares at us, expecting a show, and all I can do is sit dumbly with the hot dog glued to my palm. They probably think I'm such a Goody Two-shoes. I want to throw it, but it's just not . . . *me*. I get in trouble for reading ahead during English. Not for throwing food.

A chant starts up at the basketball table. *Chuck it! Chuck it!* My cheeks burn up under the imaginary spotlight. There's no way I can do this. I've never gotten detention in my life.

But these guys don't know that. They don't know anything about me.

They *do* know my name, though. And something about that feels strangely good.

I squeeze the hot dog and slowly stand, my heart thumping to the beat of the chant.

Chuck it! Chuck it!

California Ben wouldn't dare.

Chuck it! Chuck it!

But nobody ever noticed him.

Chuck it! Chuck it!

Sometimes, change is good.

In the far corner of the cafeteria, the lunchroom monitor, Ms. Jones, reenters the cafeteria. She leans against the wall and swipes through her phone. I'll have to be quick.

I draw back my arm, aim for the clock, and throw as hard as I can. The hot dog zips through the air, smooth as a jet, and *boings* off the 12, leaving a splotch of grease. Then it nose-dives for the vending machine, ricochets off the side, and tumbles halfway across the cafeteria like a rabid bunny.

Hunter and I cheer, along with the basketball crew. The athletes pump their fists in my honor, and I can't wipe the cheesy grin off my face.

Note to self: Chucking hot dogs is a great way to impress people.

I check to make sure Ms. Jones didn't see what just went down. Somehow she's still glued to her phone, totally oblivious to the lunchroom chaos. Thank goodness for technology.

Hunter smacks my back as I sit down. "Dude, you got six bounces! That's the most I've ever seen!"

Ellie tries to look annoyed, but her dimples betray her. "I know what I'm getting you guys next Christmas. A pack of jumbo hot dogs."

BLERRRRRRRP!

My body jolts as an air horn blasts through the cafeteria. The cheer squad jogs through the double doors at the far end of the room.

The tallest cheerleader holds a megaphone to her lips. "Heeeeey, South Fork Middle School!" Behind her, the girls shake their shiny red pom-poms.

Hunter points to Jayla, a blond cheerleader in the back row. He leans in. "There's your girl."

Fact check: Jayla's not my girl. She's way out of my league. Last week in English, I tossed a crumpled-up paper into the wastebasket and she said, "Nice shot." That's the extent of our relationship. I have no clue why Hunter has started teasing me about her.

Jayla does a high kick and lines up with her team. Her sleek ponytail flows halfway down her back like a golden waterfall. It looks so soft. And shiny. And—

Jayla catches my eye and I snap my head toward Hunter. He snorts and gives me a knowing grin. How embarrassing.

"All right!" the cheer captain yells into the megaphone. "I know you're all pumped for the BIG GAME TONIGHT!" The room erupts with applause.

"And what better way to spend your Friday night," she shouts, "than cheering on our South Fork Spuds against the Hamilton *Jackrabbits.*" She sneers the word "Jackrabbits," and the students roar back with boos. Hamilton is our school's rival. From what I've heard, their reputation is definitely deserved. Once, they scattered rabbit poop across our team's locker room. These guys are bad news.

The head cheerleader sweeps her arm toward the doorway. "And now let's give a warm welcome to our very own Steeeve the Spuuud!"

I do a facepalm. "You've got to be kidding me."

A kid in a plushy potato costume bursts through the double doors. Weak cheers and snickers fill the cafeteria. The Spud mascot hops around and pumps his twiggy arms in the air like a giant beanbag come to life. He looks like Mr. Potato Head's nephew: the same cartoonish smile and googly eyes, but no mustache. Too bad. A mustache would significantly increase his coolness factor.

"Why do I go to a school that worships my least favorite vegetable?" I say.

Ellie nudges me. "Our school founders were potato farmers. Show some respect."

Music blares from the speakers, and Steve the Spud skips down the aisles, passing out high fives like he's some kind of celebrity. A few kids slap his hand, but most shrink away like he's got a contagious disease. This whole scene is so cringeworthy. Why would anyone in their right mind agree to wear that costume?

Suddenly the mascot's foot lands on the hot dog I flung across the cafeteria. His arms flail as the hot dog rolls under his foot. He shrieks and wobbles, trying to catch his balance, and—*splat!*—flops to the floor like a pancake.

This is one of those moments where you're not supposed to laugh, but it's too funny to hold in. I mean, a potato flailing its arms, and the high-pitched scream . . . it's just too much. Hunter and I double over in laughter, along with most of the cafeteria. My hot dog—*my* hot dog—brought down the demon veggie. Today is definitely my day.

Ellie frowns. "Poor Wyatt. I hope he's not hurt."

I force myself to stop laughing. I guess I forgot there was an actual person inside that suit. "You know him?"

"Yeah, he sits by me in math."

That explains why I haven't heard of him. Ellie's a year ahead in math, so this Wyatt guy must be an eighth grader.

"I'm gonna go see how he's doing," Ellie says. She tucks her book under her arm and rushes over to Wyatt. On the other side of the cafeteria, a couple of teachers help him to his feet. It looks like he's okay. I hope so, anyway.

When the bell rings, I stand to go to English. My classroom is at the other end of the building, so I need to leave right now. I almost got a tardy yesterday. I toss my lunch into the trash bin at the end of the table. "See ya, Hunter."

"Not so fast, Mr. Hardy."

The voice comes from behind me. I whirl around and stare into the eyes of the lunchroom monitor, Ms. Jones, who is pinching a napkin-wrapped hot dog between her fingers.

2

I Really Need to Work on My Bargaining Skills

Ms. Jones adjusts her glasses. "Anything you want to tell me?"

A lump forms in my throat, but I swallow it down. I can't let her sense my fear. "Ms. Jones!" I force a smile. "Your hair looks good today. So nice and frizzy."

She frowns. Maybe frizzy is a bad thing. "I mean nice and shiny?"

"Flattery won't work. Did you throw this hot dog, yes or no?"

My smile drops, along with my stomach. It's over. I'll get detention, my parents will freak, and I definitely won't get to go to the basketball game tonight—all because of a stupid hot dog. This is so embarrassing.

I'm not ready to give up. "Aren't I innocent until proven guilty?"

She arches an eyebrow. "You're not going to make us review the video footage in the cafeteria, are you?"

Video footage? What is this, a prison?

I open my mouth, but it takes a while for anything to come out. "I didn't mean to hurt him," I finally manage. "Honest." I look her in the eye, hoping she realizes I mean it. Hoping she realizes this isn't like me.

She smirks. "Well, I'm glad you confessed, because there are no video cameras in the cafeteria. Follow me."

Dang. She's good.

I trudge behind her as we weave our way through the halls, a total walk of shame. Who else in this hallway saw me get busted? Chucking hot dogs is cool. Getting in trouble is not. You're supposed to be sneaky about it.

"Principal Jensen does not tolerate food-throwing," Ms. Jones calls over her shoulder. I wish she wouldn't talk so loud.

But wait. We're going to the principal's office? I've managed to never speak to a principal in my entire life, a streak I did not plan on breaking. I think I'm gonna be sick.

Ms. Jones has me sit in a chair by the secretary's desk as she steps into the principal's office. My ears won't stop ringing. Mom used to say that meant people were talking about you. I guess she was right.

After a few long minutes, Ms. Jones comes back out. "Principal Jensen will see you now," she says before she leaves to return to the cafeteria. My stomach lurches. Here we go. I walk to the door, turn the handle, and step inside.

I'm hit with the smell of old books and new leather. On the wall hangs a picture of Principal Jensen with his wife and daughters, two little girls with matching pigtails.

"Hello, hello!" the principal says. Against his dark brown skin, his perfect smile gleams beneath a thin mustache. I don't believe it—it's like he's actually happy to see me.

The man sitting across from him, however, is clearly not. "Hmph," he grunts. It's Coach Tudy, the gym teacher and basketball coach. What's he doing here?

"Take a seat, Ben." Principal Jensen motions to the fancy swivel chair in front of his desk. I sit and resist the urge to swivel.

Coach Tudy glares at me, his bald white head gleaming under the fluorescent lighting. He's a seriously tough guy—and his

muscles would agree—despite his hilarious last name, which is pronounced *tooty*.

I met Coach in the front office when Mom was registering me for classes on my first day of school. "You play sports?" he asked. I told him that I skateboard but not much else. "That's not a sport, boy!" he said in a voice that, at its lowest volume, could wake a corpse. "Doesn't even use a ball." Then he stomped away, shaking his head and muttering something about kids not being the same these days.

I try to ignore Coach Tudy's glare and focus on Principal Jensen instead. He clears his throat, and his mustache twitches. "I understand we had a little . . . accident in the cafeteria today?" He's acting like I'm a five-year-old who peed his pants.

"Not just a little accident," Coach Tudy says. "He tripped my star mascot!"

Star mascot? I've heard of star quarterbacks. Star basketball starters. But star mascot? Really?

Principal Jensen gives Coach an understanding nod and then looks at me. "Three years ago, we had a massive food fight in the cafeteria. One girl slipped on some Jell-O and fell into a trash can. Fractured her wrist. Since then, we take food-throwing very seriously around here."

I try not to laugh at the image of legs kicking out of the

top of a trash can. I thought food fights only happened in movies. Maybe this school is cooler than I thought.

"So," Principal Jensen says, scrunching up his face with regret, "considering your actions could have started another food fight, this could definitely warrant suspension."

"What?" I blurt. This isn't fair! I mean, it's not like I'm innocent, but suspension? That's for kids who ditch class and get into fistfights. If I get suspended my first month at a new school, I'll be forever known as a Bad Kid. I'm not brooding enough to pull that off!

Principal Jensen shrugs, slowly and dramatically. "In situations like these, we normally meet with your parents and set some behavioral goals."

My parents? They'll kill me! How can I get Principal Jensen to show some mercy? I lower my voice and widen my eyes. "Please, sir. They're already worried sick about my dog's worms. We don't want to add another thing to their plate."

Principal Jensen chortles to himself and leans back in his chair. I'm clearly not getting any sympathy here.

He doesn't get it. Back in fifth grade, my math teacher complained to my mom that I would read books during class. Books! She grounded me for two weeks. If *that* offense equaled two weeks, then *this* will equal—oh, let me do the math—forever! I'll never get to hang out with Hunter and Ellie again. Just when I was getting used to having real friends.

"I'll do anything." I widen my eyes with all the sincerity I can muster. "I messed up, but I promise it will never happen again. Isn't there anything I can do?"

"In fact, there is." Principal Jensen looks suddenly delighted. "Coach Tudy has a generous proposition for you. Take it from here, Coach."

Coach Tudy crosses his beefy arms and grunts. "When Wyatt fell, he rolled his ankle. Pretty nasty sprain, swelled up like a balloon. He'll need two weeks of rest. Maybe three."

The mascot got injured because of me? Guilt plops in my stomach like a brick.

"I want you to sub for him," Coach says. "There are four games left in the season, including the one tonight. If we make playoffs, Wyatt should be able to take over again."

"Wait. You want me to be the mascot?" Now, in a normal school, subbing for the mascot wouldn't be a huge deal, but we are the South Fork Spuds. *Spuds.* I'd have to dress up like a potato. The same potato everyone was just laughing at in the cafeteria. I wouldn't be caught dead wearing that ridiculous costume.

"I don't know," I say. "What if I led a few cheers or something? Like a school-spirit leader." Still embarrassing, but at least I could wear my own clothes.

Coach leans forward, his whistle dangling menacingly around his neck. "Are you seriously trying to bargain with me? I'm doing you a favor, kid."

"I'd just rather not wear the costume."

"It's part of the deal. Take it or leave it."

"But everyone will laugh at me—"

"Seems you like making people laugh."

"And it's a *potato*—"

"Our school founders were potato farmers," Principal Jensen cuts in.

"So I've heard." I grimace.

In middle school, it's easy to get stuck with a label, and it's nearly impossible to peel it off. I'd hate to be known as the dorky potato mascot for the rest of my school career. But I'd also hate to be known as the kid who got suspended. For the first time in my life, people seem to respect me and know who I am. I just had the whole basketball table chanting for me. I can't mess this up.

I picture everyone laughing at the Spud in the cafeteria. But I also picture Mom's disappointed face. And people whispering in the halls: *Did you hear the new kid got suspended?* The back of my neck burns at the thought.

At least as the mascot, I'll be covered up. No one has to know it's me.

"Fine. I'll do it." I hardly believe the words as they exit my mouth. "But no one can know about this. No one."

"Sure," says Coach. "Mum's the word. Now, how do you get home after school?"

"I walk."

"All right. Meet me in the gym before you head home. You'll try on the suit and we'll go over instructions."

"Yes, Coach," I grumble.

Principal Jensen clasps his hands together. "Well, well. Looks like we've found a solution that makes everyone happy. Isn't compromise wonderful?" He scribbles out a tardy pass and hands it to me. I turn to leave.

"Wait, Hardy," Coach says before I can escape. "I have your word you'll do all four games?"

"Yeah, okay."

He holds out his hand and we shake on it. My fingers crunch under his firm grip.

This might go down in history as the worst deal ever made.

3
Let the Lies Begin

When the final bell rings, I head to the gym. I've got a date with a potato suit.

I can't believe it's come to this.

Halfway down the hall, a deep voice calls after me. "Hey, Ben. Come here."

Duke Watters, the leader of the "chuck it" chant, leans against his locker and nods at me. He's the basketball team's center, and possibly the only redhead in the world who never got made fun of for his hair color. At five foot eight, he towers over the other seventh graders and likes to stick little pieces of paper in the hair of whoever's sitting in front of him during class.

Did he find out I'm the mascot? If so, I'm doomed. I wouldn't be shocked if Coach let it slip, and in a school with fewer than two hundred students, word travels faster than a hot dog flying through the air.

I draw in a deep breath and head over. Stay cool.

Duke lifts his chin. I brace for the worst.

"I didn't think you were actually gonna throw the hot dog today. That was hilarious."

Well, that was unexpected.

"Yeah," I say, trying to sound like I *didn't* just almost have a heart attack. "They give us rubber meat. What else are we supposed to do with it?"

"Dude, and when the mascot tripped . . ." He mimics the flailing arms, and I can't help but laugh. His impression is spot-on.

"Spudboy didn't know what hit him!" I say.

"Spudboy. Ha! That's got a nice ring to it."

And just like that, I've created my new nickname. It was pretty dumb to make fun of the very mascot I'm about to become.

Duke lowers his voice. "I saw Ms. Jones talking to you after lunch. Did you get busted?"

"Nah." I shrug like *no big deal,* knowing he'll think it's cooler if I snuck away uncaught. "I just complimented her hair and she let it slip."

"Smooth!" He smacks my hand, and I try to keep from wincing. Duke high-fives pretty hard.

"See that guy over there?" Duke motions down the hall to a scrawny kid with ghostly-white skin. His large orange jacket puffs out like a Cheeto. I recognize him from our English class. He called the teacher Mom the other day, and that's all I really know about him.

"Mitch, right?" I ask.

"I don't know. The weird one. I saw him pointing you out to Ms. Jones right before she tried to bust you. Thought you should know."

Really? Mitch has always seemed nicer than that. I think back to earlier in the cafeteria. I try to remember what I saw. You know what? I did see Ms. Jones go up to a kid in an orange jacket. Right before the bell rang.

What the heck? What does Mitch have against *me*? I even lent him my pencil once. Come to think of it, he never gave it back.

"What a snitch," I say.

"Mitch the Snitch!" says Duke. "Ha!"

"Maybe I should report *him* for having the world's ugliest jacket," I say. "He looks like a traffic-cone-colored marshmallow."

Duke tosses his head back and laughs like I'm a stand-up comedian. "Ah, man. It's true."

So maybe that was mean, but at least it made Duke laugh. Besides, Mitch deserves it. It's thanks to him I'm gonna have to dress like a potato. I should charge him for that pencil he borrowed. Plus interest.

Duke opens his locker, and a handful of sparkly four-leaf clovers falls to the floor. It's like a leprechaun exploded in there. The locker is stuffed with green glitter, paper clovers, and mini pom-poms.

Duke pulls out a piece of green paper and reads it:

I'd be LUCKY to go to the Winter Dance
with you.
♡ Paris

I recognize that name. She's the girl with a blue streak in her hair. She's always with Jayla.

"Dang it, Paris." Duke brushes glitter off his pants. "I'm gonna be sparkly for days."

I can't believe it. He just got asked to a dance, and he's not even fazed. If that happened to me, I'd probably pass out.

I heard there was a girl-ask-guy dance coming up, but I didn't believe anyone would actually take dates. Last year I went to my school's sixth-grade Spring Fling, and it was just a bunch of kids either standing awkwardly in the corner or jumping around.

Literally jumping. There was a bouncy house.

"Has anyone asked you yet?" Duke says, shaking off his backpack. It's weird he assumes I'm gonna get asked.

"No," I say, and to be honest, I'd rather it stay that way. Having to make conversation while attempting to dance? No thanks.

Jayla and Paris jump out from behind the corner down the hall and start cracking up. "Glitter-bombed!" yells Jayla. She's still in her red-and-black outfit from the pep rally at lunch.

They make their way toward us, and my stomach flips like I'm at the top of Splash Mountain. I can already feel my tongue swelling up.

"Hey, I gotta go," I blurt, and book it in the opposite direction. Behind me, the girls catch up to Duke and start waving the glittery clovers all over him. Close call.

With the exception of Ellie and blood relatives, my general policy is to stay clear of girls—especially ones I like. It always ends in disaster.

Evidence #1: Fifth grade. Wilson Elementary School cafeteria. Jenny Phillips said, "Hey, how are you?" and I said, "Burrito." *Burrito*. Why? Because I was eating a burrito, and it was the first word that came to mind. We never spoke again.

Evidence #2: Sixth grade. Roosevelt Middle School hallway. Natasha Mendoza waved at me. When I waved back, I spilled my water bottle. Worse, the water splashed in a very unfortunate place, and Jimmy Rogers told everyone I had peed my pants. I'll never forgive Jimmy.

Evidence #3: Last semester. Ms. Carola's math class. Sunny Matthews showed me her perfect test score. I tried to high-five her and accidentally hit her in the face.

Clearly, talking to Jayla is not worth the risk.

I check my phone for the time. I need to get to the gym now. No more distractions.

When I step through the door to the courtyard, I immediately spot Ellie and Hunter peering into a trash can. Ellie's hard to miss because of the giant cello strapped to her back. Her voice rings out. "I'm not reaching in there! You do it!"

I know I said no more distractions, but if someone's

gonna reach into that trash can, I want to witness it firsthand. Plus, I need to tell Ellie I can't walk home today. I can't believe I almost forgot.

I make a beeline for them. "Hey, guys. Looking for treasure? Or should I say . . ."—I pause for dramatic effect—"*trash*-ure?"

Hunter snickers, but Ellie doesn't look amused. "Hunter threw my phone in the trash," she sputters. "In the trash!"

"By accident!" he squeaks.

"How do you throw a phone away by accident?" I ask.

"I was throwing away a fruit-snacks wrapper and forgot I was holding it." He shrugs like it's the most obvious explanation in the world.

I hook my thumbs under my backpack straps. "Well, wish I could help, but I'm kind of in a rush. And, Ellie—I can't walk home today. I have to help Coach Tudy with some . . . chores." Not the best lie, but at least it's partly true.

"Chores? What, like some punishment for throwing the hot dog?"

"Yeah, exactly. Like a punishment."

Ellie sets her cello down and uses Hunter's phone as a flashlight to peer through the hole at the top of the trash can. Her black braid dangles dangerously close to an open carton of milk. "You'll have to tell us about it at the game tonight."

"Oh, and Misty had her foal," says Hunter, "so I'm not on pregnancy watch anymore. I can come too!"

The game tonight. Shoot.

I scratch my neck. "About that. I'm so sorry, you guys, but I can't go."

Ellie freezes, and for a second I think she's gonna drop Hunter's phone in the trash. The sad look on her face makes me feel like the worst friend in the world.

"Why not?" she asks.

"I'm super grounded."

"Grounded?" Hunter leans against the trash can. "How are you already grounded?"

"The school called my mom and she texted me. She said, 'Ben, you're super grounded.'" I really need a better game plan next time I'm gonna lie.

This might be the first real secret I've kept from Hunter and Ellie. I mean, it's not like I've told them every detail of my life. They don't know I used to skateboard. They don't know I didn't make my last school's basketball team. They don't know I watch reruns of *My Little Pony* with my ten-year-old sister when I'm bored and have nothing else to do. But if they asked me about any of those things directly, I wouldn't lie to their faces. (Except maybe about *My Little Pony.*)

But hiding the fact that I'm the mascot is truly necessary. I need this to blow over quickly and quietly. Besides, Hunter couldn't keep a secret if his lips were duct-taped shut. He can't even keep his own secrets. He showed up to school the other day admitting to everyone that he forgot to wear deodorant and had to rub hand sanitizer on his armpits instead.

Yep. Hand sanitizer.

I'm already dreading the game tonight, but if Hunter told people it was *me* in there? I'd die of embarrassment. I can see it on the evening news: LOCAL BOY DIES IN POTATO SUIT. POSSIBLE SUFFOCATION.

Ellie would probably keep my secret. But she'd probably *also* go all school-spirit on me and critique my performances. What if I'm the worst mascot ever, and she doesn't want to be friends anymore? I'm thinking that what she doesn't know won't kill her.

"How long you grounded for?" Hunter asks.

The final game of the season is two Fridays away. Then Wyatt can be mascot again if we make playoffs. "Two weeks and I'll be free."

"Could be worse," he says. Little does he know.

Ellie resumes looking in the trash for her phone. "I still want you to buy a game-day shirt, you know."

"I will," I say. "I promise." It's the least I can do. And compared with the costume I'm about to try on, the shirt suddenly doesn't seem so bad.

"Aha!" She flings her arms around like she's swatting invisible flies. "Hunter, I see it! Right there, under the milk carton. Get it!"

Hunter sticks his arm into the trash can and scrunches up his face. "It's all *slimy* in here!" He yanks his arm out and pretends to barf.

"Come on!" Ellie nudges him. "Try again!"

I try not to laugh for Ellie's sake, but a snort comes out anyway. As much as I'd enjoy watching Hunter reach into the trash can again, Coach might call off our deal if he thinks I stood him up.

"Guys, I really have to go. Good luck getting the phone out," I say, and rush to the gym.

4

The Felty Suit of Doom

The South Fork gym building sits far in the back of the school, past a couple of portable trailers used for art classes. It definitely looks in need of an upgrade. Hundreds of black spots dot the gray stucco—wads of chewing gum that have probably been there since Coach Tudy started working here like thirty years ago.

I walk through two sets of doors and onto the empty court. The inside's almost as sad as the outside: rickety bleachers, ratty nets, scuffed floor. The red banners are impressive, though. They line three of the four walls, each announcing a South Fork achievement. GIRLS' SOCCER CHAMPIONS, CROSS-COUNTRY STATE QUALIFIERS. The latest banner proudly announces BOYS' BASKETBALL STATE RUNNERS-UP. I heard that the poop-scattering

Jackrabbits took first last year. And the year before that.

The metal doors clang, and in marches Coach Tudy, sporting a long-sleeved shirt that says WINNERS NEVER QUIT, QUITTERS NEVER WIN.

"Hardy! Follow me," he orders. No time for pleasantries with this guy.

I follow him to a medium-sized storage closet in the hall. The door squeaks open like dying mice. A single dim light bulb shines over a mess of brooms, mop buckets, and cleaning supplies. On a hook in the corner, the potato suit bulges out from the wall like a firm pillow.

Coach Tudy snatches the suit off the hook. He holds on to the head and thrusts the body at me with a "Go ahead—see how it fits."

I stare blankly at the blotchy, brown fabric. "How do I put it on?"

"There's two leg holes. Don't you dress yourself, boy? Step in, one leg at a time."

I dig around the cushiony inside of the suit with my left foot until it slips through the leg hole. I do the same with my right foot, and then pull the costume up to my chest. It literally smells like moldy old potatoes.

"Put your arms through the armholes," Coach says.

I slide my hands through the itchy felt fabric. My arms hang down like a gorilla's, arching out from my body. The sad part is, a gorilla costume would be much preferable to this.

"Time for the head." Coach Tudy places the mud-colored mound over me like he's helping a child put on an oversized helmet. Inside, it feels muggy, like the last guy's sweat never fully evaporated. It's dark, as if I wormed my way into a real overgrown potato.

In front of my eyes rests a black mesh screen—the opening of the Spud's smiling mouth. I can see out, but no one can see in, and my view is limited to a hand-sized rectangle.

"Secure the head," orders Coach Tudy. "There's a latch on each side that snaps onto the suit." I reach up to find the latches, and Coach guides my hand to click them into place. "That's so the head doesn't fall off when you take a spill," he says.

"*When* I take a spill?"

"And you're gonna need brown tights. I'll tell Wyatt to drop his off in here before the game."

"Hold up. I am *not* wearing tights. Especially tights another dude has worn. That's gross." I cross my arms in determination.

"Bring your own, then."

I scoff. "Like I have tights! I'll wear basketball shorts."

Coach's bushy eyebrows knit together. "The Spud doesn't wear *basketball shorts*. He'd look ridiculous. He wears tights. He's always worn tights. Do you understand?"

This is clearly one issue on which he won't budge. "Fine," I grumble. "I'll bring my own."

He relaxes. "Now, I want you to understand your importance to the team. The word 'mascot' is French for 'lucky charm.' You bring luck to the team, but only if your heart's in it."

"You really believe that?"

"'Course I do. Seen it myself. The mascot lifts morale. Energy in the crowd brings energy to the team. Basketball is a game of momentum."

"Momentum? Isn't that what cheerleaders are for?"

"Cheerleaders help, but without the mascot, they're missing half the magic."

It'll be easier to agree with everything he says so I can get out of this potato prison as soon as humanly possible. "You know, Coach, come to think of it, you're totally right."

"'Course I am. Now step into the hall and let's see you dance."

Seriously?

I back out of the closet. The bottom edge of the suit hangs a few inches above my knees, making it hard to move. I wiggle my arms and sway back and forth.

"Pathetic," Coach barks, like he thinks he's a judge on one of those television talent shows.

I clench my teeth and wiggle my arms faster, even throwing in spirit fingers for kicks.

"Do it like this." He punches his arms rhythmically and kicks his legs out to the sides.

I snort. "What, were you like a mascot or something?"

He frowns. "Laugh all you want, boy. There's no shame in being a mascot."

Hold up. This is too good. "Coach, were you seriously a mascot? Didn't you play sports? You're the coach."

"'Course I played sports. But I was the mascot in my off-seasons. The crowds loved me."

"I bet they did!" Oh, how I'd love to go back in time to see that.

"So, tonight your job is to pump up the crowd during time-outs. Let's stick with dancing for now. At halftime, we might call you up to shoot some hoops." He rubs his chin. "You any good at that?"

"My layup stinks, but my free throw's all right."

"Can you juggle?"

"It's been a while." In California, Dad and I would juggle with the oranges that fell off the trees in our backyard. It's too cold for orange trees here.

"What about handstands?"

"I think I can do one against the wall."

He shakes his head. "I'm gonna need you to practice. Come up with your own routines if you want. I hear the Google is chock-full of mascot ideas these days."

"The Google. I think I've heard of it. I'll look it up."

"Good. Now, you wanna go practice shooting hoops?"

"It's okay. I think I can manage." I really should practice, but if I get home too late, Mom will want to know where I was.

"If you're sure." He tosses me a set of keys that jingle as they fly through the air. "Come in any time after school to practice. Can I trust you to be responsible with those keys?"

"Yes, Coach." I'm surprised he trusts me at all after I injured his star mascot. I'll have to be really careful not to lose these keys.

I take off the headpiece, which feels like exiting a sauna. I reenter the closet and hang it on its hook.

"Any last questions?" Coach asks.

"Just one." I'm dying to know. "What kind of mascot were you?"

He folds his arms and stares me down as if daring me to laugh. "Winchester the Chipmunk."

I channel all my inner energy to keep a straight face. I raise my eyebrows, and in my most sincere voice I say, "I bet you were a wonderful mascot."

Coach's eyes cloud over, and across his face spreads the closest thing to a smile I've ever seen him wear. "I remember the state championships in 1979. I had the crowd roaring." He chuckles softly. "I learned how to do a back handspring. My signature move was nibbling on the other team's mascot."

He snaps out of cheery-chipmunk land and back to the dingy closet. "Okay, Hardy, be ready to perform at the next four games. We play tonight, next Wednesday, the following Tuesday, and that Friday."

"Wednesday, Tuesday, Friday," I repeat.

"Be here early to change. And remember, you're gonna have to put your heart into this. Even if our team falls behind, you never quit. Bring out the positive energy. You're our lucky charm."

I have the strongest urge to roll my eyes all the way to the back of my head, but I hold it together. "I won't let you down, Coach. I'll be the best Spud I can be."

5
My Grand Debut

Operation: Mascot Transformation

Time: 5:00 p.m. sharp

*Cue *Mission: Impossible* theme*

I arrive at school a good hour before the game. My parents think I'm here early to help prepare the concession food. Dad would sometimes volunteer at the concession stand at my old school, which is where I got the idea. He offered to come help tonight, but Mom needed him home since they're sanding down the kitchen cabinets. They bought a fixer-upper and have been working on some project or other since we moved in.

A fresh layer of snow blankets the campus, with no tracks in sight. Good. Fewer witnesses. If anyone sees me lurking around, they'll know I'm not grounded. They might piece it all together. They might spread the word.

No one can be trusted.

I pull up my hood and speed-walk toward the gym. Suddenly a group of girls exits the building to my right. They wear matching red sweatpants and jackets with the Spud logo on them.

Oh no. The cheerleaders.

I duck behind the nearest tree and pretend to text. *Please let no one see me,* I silently pray. *Please.*

Not a minute later, Jayla pops up to my right. "Hey, Ben."

I drop my phone in the snow. So much for the prayer.

With shaky hands, I dig the phone out of the snow and wipe it on my jeans.

"Oops," Jayla says. She turns around and waves her friends on. "If it got wet, I heard it helps to put it in a bowl of rice."

"Do you have any rice?" I ask. Dumbest question *ever.* Why would she have rice?

She laughs, so I guess she thought I was joking. "Why are you at school so late?"

She's already onto me. "I'm . . . homeworking." I inwardly cringe.

"Like, you stayed to do homework with a teacher?"

At least she's giving me material to work with. "Yeah. That."

She plays with the zipper on her jacket. "The team and I were making a banner for the game tonight."

"That's awesome."

She shows off her red fingertips. "We got to use finger paints."

"That's awesome. I bet it'll look super awesome." Ugh. I must be stunning her with my *awesome* vocabulary.

I examine my phone, tapping on the different apps. Instagram, check. CloudGerbil, check. Everything seems to be working fine.

Jayla's still here. Why is she still here?

She circles her toe in the snow. "Duke said you haven't been asked to the dance yet. You dance?"

No, I think. But instead I say, "Yes." I really need to work on my brain-to-mouth connection.

"Cool." She smiles, and light bounces off her lip gloss like a million tiny diamonds. "Well, I have to run home and eat before the game. You going?"

"Yeah," I say. It's true. I'll be the one in the potato suit.

"You should come say hi to me during warm-ups."

"Yeah, yeah. Of course."

What am I thinking? I can't say hi to her before the game! But before I can correct myself, she's walking away, her long ponytail swinging behind her.

What was that all about? And why can't I act normal?

I shove the thoughts out of my head. There's no time to think about it. I have to get to the gym before people start showing up.

I jog the rest of the way, watching the area for more witnesses. Once I safely reach the janitor's closet, it's time for the second phase of the operation: get dressed.

I replace my jeans with the brown leggings I dug out of my little sister Abby's dresser while she was downstairs making a smoothie. She's half a foot shorter than me, but the fabric stretches surprisingly far. Not uncomfortable, either, I've gotta admit.

Time to face my worst nightmare. The potato suit hangs in the corner, mocking me with its googly eyes. I tug it off its hook, and it knocks over a broom, which whacks me on the back of the head. Figures. The suit has it in for me, I swear. After all, it is a potato—aka the starchy root of all evil. I sense hatred in its eyes and glare back to assure it the feeling is mutual.

I pull the suit up to my chest, slip my arms through the armholes, and buckle on the head. Showtime.

A question hits me as I scuffle down the hall: What should I do if anyone tries talking to me? Disguise my voice? Yes. I can make my voice go pretty deep. Throw in an accent? No. Too risky. And if they ask my name?

After some thought, I settle on the name Doug. Yes, Doug is a nice, safe name. A name quite suitable for a potato, if you think about it. Plus, I don't know anyone named Doug.

I waddle down the court to the wooden bench on the sideline. It creaks when I sit, and I almost topple backward. Sitting in a potato suit isn't easy. It's like trying to balance with a beach ball strapped to your butt.

About fifteen minutes later, fans start trickling into

the gym, filling the stands with specks of red and black. I stay seated like a lump, reliving the awkwardness of being alone at a lunch table on my first day of school, something I never want to experience again.

Now that there's time to think, I replay the conversation with Jayla over in my head. "You dance?" she said. Is there a chance—even the teeniest sliver of a chance—that she's thinking of asking me? That's kind of what it sounded like.

What is it with today? First I go to the principal's office. Then Duke acts like we're buddies. Then Jayla goes out of her way to talk to me. Throw in the fact that I'm currently in a potato suit, and I'd say today is hands-down the weirdest day of my life. I imagine sparkly clovers falling out of my own locker—or something cooler, like splat balls—and the funny thing is, I'm not hyperventilating thinking about it. I'm actually kind of excited. Maybe California Ben couldn't handle going to a dance. But Idaho Ben just might.

Soon the gym is full. The happy chatter of the crowd echoes off the walls, and the band belts an energetic tune. "Eye of the Tiger"? It's hard to tell since they aren't very good.

The song ends and the cheer squad leads a chant:

SPUDS, NOT DUDS! SOUR CREAM OF THE CROP!
WE MASH THE COMPETITION AND WE NEVER STOP!

Jayla smiles at the front of the line, her ponytail shining under the bright lights. She scans the crowd from left to right like she's searching for someone. Could it be me?

The butterflies in my stomach need to chill out. I'm reading too much into things. Even if she is looking for me, I am a total jerk for standing her up. If she was ever planning to ask me to the dance, she's probably not anymore.

Ellie, Hunter, and a couple of other girls sit in the section to the right. Hunter's obviously trying to impress Ellie's curly-haired friend. He keeps folding his arms while flexing to show off his muscles. Oldest trick in the book.

On the opposite side of the gym, the Hamilton Jackrabbits have a decent crowd of their own, which isn't surprising. The Jackrabbits are known for being super competitive. I bet their basketball players are like mini celebrities.

A furry white figure hops up and down their bleachers. I squint. It can't be.

And yet it is. The Jackrabbits brought along their mascot. And he's not a cute, cuddly bunny, but rather a creepy Easter rabbit, with red eyes shining out of his foam head. He points right at me and pounds his fists together. Is that a threat? I shudder.

The rabbit bounces around giving high fives like he's the Energizer Bunny turned to the dark side. With all his school spirit, he's totally making me look bad. I almost get up to high-five fans too, but I remember how most of the Spud's high fives went unreceived at the cafeteria rally, and I stay glued to the bench.

"So, you're the new Spud, huh?" A kid with crutches stands next to my bench. His hair is braided into cornrows, and every other row is dyed red. Who could this be?

Oh, wait. Crutches . . .

"I'm Wyatt," he says.

"'Sup. I'm Doug." Thank goodness I planned an alias.

"I'm the usual mascot," Wyatt says. He flashes me a smile. The red and black rubber bands on his braces match his cornrows. "Thanks for covering for me. Being the Spud is pretty fun. I think you'll like it."

This dude clearly has a warped sense of fun. At least he doesn't seem to be too bummed out about his ankle being hurt. Which is kind of, sort of, totally my fault.

He taps my bench with one of his crutches. "You get a courtside seat. You get to dance around, pump everyone up." His smile stays plastered on his face. Seriously, who brainwashed this kid?

"Watch out for these guys, though." He nods at the Jackrabbit fans. "Once, they showered me with potato peels."

Well, that explains the suit's moldy potato smell.

I keep my voice deep. "I'll keep an eye out. Thanks, man."

"Good luck, Doug." Wyatt hobbles off to join his friends. One of them waves a sign that says WE'RE SPUD-TACULAR! and another WE BUTTER WIN! I gotta admit, that one's pretty good. I have a weakness for puns.

On the guest side, the signs are less . . . positive. One sign shouts BOIL 'EM, MASH 'EM, STICK 'EM IN A STEW! Another says PREPARE TO GET FRENCH FRIED!!!

The starting five gather at center court for the jump ball, and a shrill whistle cuts through the air. Duke, being a good three inches taller than the Jackrabbits' center, easily tips the ball to our side. It's game on.

Player thirteen, Cole Evans, makes the first shot—a three-pointer—to thunderous applause. But neither team keeps the lead for long. Ellie was right about the Jackrabbit games being intense. Too intense. During the first quarter, one of their players swings his elbow into a Spuds player's stomach, sending him doubling over. The ref calls a flagrant foul and kicks him out of the game.

During the first time-out, I face the crowd and pump my arms to the music. *Whoomp, there it is. Whoomp, there it is*. I always thought this song was mildly annoying, but now I know I'll hate it forever.

I feel like an idiot, but no one seems to be paying attention to me anyway. Coach was wrong—I'm not influencing the game at all. I could disappear and no one would notice. I could probably even burst into flames and no one would notice. For once in my life, it feels wonderful to be completely ignored.

At halftime, the announcer—an eighth-grade kid with a radio-worthy voice—calls me onto the court.

"Ladies and gentlemen," he yells into the mic. "We have selected one lucky fan to challenge Steve the Spud in a free-throw shoot-out!"

An administrator leads out this stocky little kid, maybe six years old, wearing an oversized baseball hat. I waddle up to him and reach out to shake his hand.

"Good luck," I say.

"You're goin' down," he sneers.

Oh, so that's how it's gonna be, then?

The kid shoots first. He misses with a total airball. Ha! The announcer tosses me the ball next. I dribble it a couple of times and step onto the free-throw line, ready to show this punk up.

Then something hits the back of my suit. I hear it on the padding—a little clop. It clops again. Then again. Is someone hitting me with small pellets?

Please, not rabbit poop. Please, please, please. I brace myself for the worst and slowly turn around.

6

Bunny vs. Potato: The Ultimate Showdown

I'm face to face with the Jackrabbit mascot, who's holding a carton of Tater Tots in his furry paws. Where did he even get those? This guy really came prepared. Prepared to torture me, that is. I step back and feel one of the tots squish under my tennis shoes. At least it's not rabbit poop.

The Jackrabbit jogs backward a few paces. He wiggles his shoulders as if to say, *I'm only getting warmed up.* He scrapes the ground with his feet like a bull, and then charges. Before I can dodge, he belly-bumps me. I topple over and hit the court with a muted thud.

The Jackrabbit somersaults away as I kick my legs in the air like a flipped-over turtle. The guest section bursts into laughter while the home fans gasp and boo—though I'm pretty sure I hear snickers coming from the home crowd too.

All right, floor. Feel free to swallow me whole. Anytime now.

The ref chases the Jackrabbit around the gym, and all I can do is lie here, helpless. What would Jayla think if she could see through my costume? Probably that I'm a dorky klutz. In my defense, it's hard to keep your balance when you have the waist size of an adult manatee.

Finally the ref catches the demon bunny by the fur of his neck and ejects him from the game with a sharp blow of the whistle. The Jackrabbit cartwheels out the open doorway like some kind of hero.

The ref grabs my hand and helps me to my feet. My head reels. I waddle back to my bench in shame, and a few nice people clap to make me feel better.

It doesn't work.

Everyone's ready to move on, and the game resumes—Spuds 42, Jackrabbits 40.

Our team quickly falls behind when a lanky Hamilton player shoots a three-pointer in the first minute of the second half. His teammate steals the ball and scores again. The Spuds miss their next shot, and the Jackrabbits bring it back for another shot. Our team is now down by five.

Coach Tudy looks absolutely bewildered as the guest section pounds their fists in the air. *De-fense!* they chant. *De-fense!*

Coach calls a time-out.

After my tumbling-over act, the last thing I want to do is dance. But what choice do I have, unless I want to look like a poor sport? I try to punch and kick, but my limbs feel like wet spaghetti.

"All right, boys," I overhear Coach say to the huddle. "We have to break their momentum."

Momentum. It suddenly becomes obvious I have broken ours.

After a short pep talk, our team returns to the court, ready to make their run. We manage a few two-pointers, but the Jackrabbits are rocking it. They shoot three-pointer after three-pointer as their fans holler and stomp. We're getting pummeled. Destroyed. Annihilated.

With twenty seconds left, the score is 71–48, Jackrabbits. The looks on our players' faces seem to say, *Why bother trying?* Their energy has been vacuum-sucked out of them. They run like they're wading through water. I know how they feel. I can't even muster the energy to get up off my bench.

The final buzzer sounds with a score of 73–48. A Jackrabbit victory.

The home bleachers are silent. Meanwhile the guest section stomps and yells, creating a thunderstorm on the other side of the gym. I wish they'd stomp hard enough that those rickety bleachers would collapse under their obnoxious little feet.

Our fans don't stick around much longer. Ellie and Hunter look pretty bummed as they shuffle out the door. I'd like to get out of here too, but if I stand, someone might push me over again. The home fans probably hate me, and to be honest, I don't blame them. Our team was playing great until my major fail.

Coach Tudy orders the players to the locker room and then remains standing at the team bench with both hands behind his bald head like he's holding it in place. I can't read his expression. Anger? Disappointment? Acceptance? Once the gym empties, he turns his head toward me so slowly I can almost hear his neck creak, like one of those creepy dolls in the horror movies. I'm not confused by his expression anymore. Anger. Definitely anger.

He marches toward me, plunks down on the bench, and speaks firmly. "Son. We need to talk about your mascotting."

He's using a "disappointed father" tone of voice, which is good, because I was expecting something more along the lines of "raging Hulk." My shoulders relax a little.

Coach stares into my eyes, or rather into the mesh screen covering my eyes. "I'm not blaming you for our loss, but I think tonight was a good example of how a mascot can really sway a game. Did you see the energy of those Jackrabbits?"

I roll my safely concealed eyes. "Yeah, but that was just because their stupid bunny knocked me over. And I'm pretty sure potato harassment is illegal in the state of Idaho."

Coach huffs. "That kid's a jerk. I'm not saying to do what he did. But at the beginning of the game, where were you?"

"On the bench." I lower my foam-encapsulated head.

"Their mascot was interacting with the fans, hopping, cartwheeling—"

"Well, his suit lets him actually move. In case you

forgot, I'm Steve the Spud. If I tried a cartwheel, I'd fall on the floor and just lie there. Like a speed bump."

We sit in silence for a while. "You know," Coach says. "It's not an easy job you got. When I was Winchester the Chipmunk, sometimes the other mascots would tug on my tail." He shakes his head like he still holds a grudge. "I tugged them right back on their ears, every time."

I squint. "So you're saying to use physical violence when necessary?"

He chuckles and claps me on the back. "I'm saying you should never give up. No matter how bad things get. Winners never quit, and quitters never win."

"You stole that saying from your T-shirt."

"The T-shirt makers stole that saying from me."

I smile a little. "Can't argue with that."

"Look," Coach says. "Our team hasn't taken state since my first year of coaching. That's twenty-two years. They told me I could retire this year—you know what I said? I'm not quitting till I see us take state again. If I'm here till I'm ninety-two, so be it."

I can totally see it: Coach hobbling down the sidelines, ordering players around with his cane and cheering so loud his dentures fall out.

He stands. "There's three games left. We need to win at least two to make playoffs. If you wanna call off the deal, I won't stop you. But I really think you can help us win. You just gotta put in some effort."

"How can I help us win if the whole school thinks I'm a dork? I heard the crowd. They were laughing at me."

"By next game they won't even remember. You'll win 'em back."

I look up. "You really think so?

"I know so. You set your mind on something, and nothing can get in your way. Not even a jerk-faced rabbit."

I hesitate. Part of me wants to quit, but I don't want to let Coach down, especially now that he's being so nice to me. Besides, if I call off our deal, suspension will be calling my name.

I square my shoulders. "Okay. I'll practice for next time, Coach."

And I honestly intend to.

• • •

Back in the janitor's closet, I unlatch the headpiece and set it on a trash bag filled with rags. I draw in a breath of fresh air. Man, it feels good to be out of that potato helmet.

Everyone's left the gym, and the building has gone to

sleep, lights dimmed and doors locked. It's spooky to be at school so late, like the ghosts of teachers past might be roaming the halls.

I'll have to explain to Mom and Dad why I took so long getting home. I can't use the concession-stand excuse. If they thought I was still packing it up, they'd assume we were shorthanded and insist on helping out next time. How about *I stopped by the gas station to get Slurpees with Hunter and Ellie*? Believable enough.

I hate lying, but my parents can't know I'm the mascot. Especially Mom. She takes being supportive way too far. Once, she got banned from my Little League games for arguing with the coach to let me bat. If she knew I was the mascot, she'd arrive early for a front-row seat and wave around a homemade sign that said WE LOVE STEVE THE SPUD! She'd probably even draw little hearts all over the poster, as if I needed more embarrassment. Someone might recognize her, and my secret would be out. Any chance I had of ever being cool would be totally and completely shot. I think of one of the words on my vocabulary list this week. "Pariah." An outcast.

I'm kneeling down to untie my shoes when the light bulb above my head starts flickering on and off. This is the definition of creepy. Last thing I want is to finish changing in the dark.

Squeak. Pause. *Squeak.* Pause. *Squeak.*

The sound comes from the outside hall. Footsteps. I could've sworn everyone was out of the building. Am I being stalked? Was I right about dead teachers' ghosts haunting the school at night?

I twist the metal doorknob to make sure it's locked. It is. I'll be safe from a stalker. Not so much from a ghost.

Squeak. Pause. *Squeak.* Pause. *Squeak.*

I stay still as a mannequin, not wanting to knock over a mop or ram into the shelf of cleaning supplies behind me. The footsteps squeak closer and closer, louder and louder, and then, suddenly, they stop. Right outside the door.

Clink, clink.

Keys jangle as the mystery person prepares to enter my sanctuary. I have to find a hiding spot. But I'm in this bulky suit. Hiding is impossible. Unless . . .

With lightning speed, I lie down in the corner, snatch the bag of rags, and empty it over my legs and face. I wiggle my arms into the suit and cross them over my chest. Now I'll look like an empty costume in the corner. Nothing to see here.

I take a deep breath as the lock clicks, the handle turns, and the door creaks open.

7
This Is Why I Hate Surprises

I hold my breath under the rag pile as the footsteps squeak their way inside. The intruder walks past me and rummages through the shelf of cleaning supplies. It must be the janitor.

As he searches the shelf for way longer than seems necessary, I realize I can't hold my breath forever. Carefully, I breathe through my nose. *Bleh.* The rags smell like dog puke.

The janitor swishes open a garbage bag and begins to stuff it with rags—starting with the pile right above my face.

The load above me lightens as he scoops it up. He reaches for a third fistful of rags but grabs my chin, which is when, I assume, he realizes he's touching human flesh.

"*AGHHHHHHHHH!*" The rags in his arms shoot up

in the air and rain down. He probably thinks he's discovered a dead body that someone stuffed in the closet for safekeeping. Not a bad place to hide a corpse, if you ask me.

I shake the remaining rags off my head and sit up. I'm shocked to see not a janitor, but a boy my own age. "Wait. Mitch?"

Mitch the Snitch from English class gapes at me like I literally rose from the dead. What's he doing here?

"Ben?" He pants like a scared Chihuahua and runs a hand through his short hair. "Why are you on the floor?"

"I was sleeping." With dirty rags over my face. Obviously.

"Sleeping?" His breath steadies and his lips tighten. "Why didn't you turn off the light, then?"

"I'm afraid of the dark."

"Why are you in the potato suit?"

"It keeps me warm."

"Why—"

"Okay, no more questions. I should be the one asking, Why are *you* here?"

He whispers, "Don't tell anyone, but this closet is actually a portal to another dimension."

I slump into the corner. "Is that a joke?"

"Just trying to give an answer that's as believable as yours." He looks proud of his little comeback. I'm not in the mood for this.

"Rub it in, why don't you?" I motion to my plushy belly. "Isn't it obvious? I'm the mascot. I was hiding. Happy?"

His face softens. "Hey, I'm sorry. I didn't mean to—"

"Forget it." I kick a mop bucket. "And it's your fault, too. Duke told me how you ratted me out to Ms. Jones."

"Oh man." He stares at the floor, his reaction alone proving his guilt. "I'm so sorry. It's just, Ms. Jones . . . she was all up in my face, and I have the hardest time lying, and . . ."

Is he seriously going to cry? I refuse to feel pity. Not when I'm the one in a potato suit. "What's done is done," I say. Anything to stop the blubbering. "Just please don't tell anybody about this. So, why are you here?"

He sniffs. "I'm cleaning up after the game."

"What, like a janitor?"

"Yeah. My dad is Larry, the head janitor." He perks up a little. "You know, the one with the cool beard."

Yeah, I know Larry. He confiscated my Mountain Dew in the cafeteria last week. Soda is banned at South Fork Middle School for reasons I'll never understand. They should ban something actually harmful, like the freakishly bouncy hot dogs that may or may not include radioactive material.

Mitch shrugs. "He lets me help out for my allowance. I'm saving up to buy a quadcopter drone. You heard of that?"

"Uh. No."

Then he goes on for way too long about all the drones he wants and their colors and their features and . . . you get the picture. I guess they're like really expensive remote-control helicopters with cameras. It's weird he's so chatty, seeing as I've never heard him talk much before. Honestly, the whole conversation kind of blurs together, and I just nod and hum in agreement while thinking about how I really want to get home to take a much-needed shower.

I finish taking off the suit and then cut in. "That's really cool, Mitch. Hey, I gotta get home. My mom'll be worried."

He grabs a broom. "Yeah, okay. Maybe I'll see you in here again next game. It's next Wednesday, right?"

"Yeah."

He reaches for the doorknob.

"Hey, Mitch." I stare him down. "You seriously can't tell anyone about this, okay? It's really important that no one finds out."

He nods solemnly. "Your secret's safe with me."

A shiver runs down my spine. My fate rests in the hands of Mitch the Snitch.

• • •

Being fake grounded stinks.

On Saturday night, while others are probably out with friends doing things like playing laser tag or watching movies, I'm stuck in my room, lounging on my beanbag and waiting for the turkey loaf in my stomach to digest. (Yes, turkey loaf. My mom has discovered meat loaf's evil twin.)

And just to rub it in, I get a text from Hunter: Wanna come over for family game night?

And I do. But I can't.

Me: Sorry, dude. Still grounded.

I went to Hunter's family game night last weekend, and it was awesome. His five sisters seem so nice and polite, but give them a deck of cards and they turn into fire-breathing dragons. The six-year-old, Regina, nearly decapitated me with an Uno card. It was the most fun I'd had in a really long time.

If Hunter finds out I'm lying to him, will he ever invite me back?

Mom peeks her head in the door.

"Mom, you gotta knock! I could be changing!"

"Oh, oh, oh!" She steps out and raps three times. "May I come in?"

"You may."

She reenters, wearing gray sweatpants and her long hair tied up in a bun. She and Dad were painting the front door this afternoon, so her T-shirt has some dark blue speckles. Everyone always says I look like Mom, which is weird because she's a girl, but I guess we have the same brown hair and thick eyebrows.

"Want to watch a movie with me and Abby?" Mom says. In her arms, our puppy, Buster, sticks his tongue out and gives me a toothy dog smile.

"Which one?"

Mom belts in her horrible opera voice, *"The hills are aliiiiiive, with the sound of muuuuusic."*

Despite my bad mood, I can't help but smile.

"Why don't you invite Hunter over?" Mom says. "And that nice girl—what's her name? Ellie? I'll make popcorn."

"Nah," I say. "That movie's like three hours long."

She lifts Buster's paws and speaks in her high-pitched dog voice. "Please, Ben! I like your friends."

"They're busy tonight."

"That's too bad," she says, and I can sense worry in her eyes, like she thinks I'm losing my friends or something. She doesn't know it, but I'm worried too.

"Maybe I'll come down later," I say, so she stops looking so sad. "I have some studying I have to do." Mascot studies, that is.

She eyes me suspiciously, because really, who studies on a Saturday night? "If you'd rather, Dad's in the basement watching the game."

"Okay, maybe. Thanks." Dad used to always watch movies with the rest of the family, but lately he's seemed more interested in the Lakers. I guess I can't blame him. They're his only connection to California now. He probably misses it there too.

After Mom leaves, it's time to get down to business. Coach is counting on me to do better next time. *I* am counting on me to do better next time. But where do I even start?

I pull up YouTube on my phone and search "cool mascots."

Jackpot. Dozens of mascot videos pop up on my screen. I'm bound to find some inspiration here.

I grab a pillow and get comfy on the beanbag. First up, Bango the Buck backflips off the top of a twenty-foot ladder and makes a slam dunk. Perfect execution.

Next, Jazz Bear rides a firework-spewing motorcycle across the court. I'd pay big bucks for a motorcycle like that one day.

Then comes Gnash the Wolf, who drops from the ceiling suspended by a harness and swings across his hockey rink like he's Tarzan on ice.

The crowds are going wild for these guys. They aren't dorky. They're heroes.

Too bad I'm not up for backflipping off a ladder. I don't have a driver's license or a motorcycle. And I don't think the school budget allows for a harness. (I'll have to ask Coach.)

A video suggestion pops up that says MASCOT FAILS in big capital letters.

Should I? Watching this can't be good for my morale. But I've gotta know what stunts to avoid.

First I watch a hawk front-flip off a springboard. His beak gets caught on the basketball rim, and he flops to the ground. I think he broke a wing.

Next, a dinosaur Rollerblades down the bleachers. He trips and face-plants his blow-up raptor head on the court.

Then a duck leaps over a pit of fire, only to have his tail go up in flames.

No springboards. No Rollerblades. No fire pits. Got it.

I watch another video. Then another. There's the dancing banana from Florida. The pickle from North Carolina. The fighting okra from Mississippi.

It's comforting to know I'm not the only one forced to dress up like food out there.

Before I know it, it's ten o'clock, and even though I've found zero stunts that I could pull off in real life, something inside me has changed. Because I, Ben Hardy, am a member of the greater global mascot community. And we never quit.

It seems the key to being a mascot is having no shame. No matter how dorky their costumes, they own it. No matter how bad they fail, they shake it off. And the crowd forgets about it. They really do.

Yeah, the duck got (literally) roasted. But the next game, he's making trick shots to thunderous applause.

Yeah, dino dude face-flopped. But there are other videos of him doing push-ups and pretending to eat the cheerleaders.

Their failures don't stick to them forever.

I let that rabbit belly-bump me down. I broke my team's momentum. But next game I'll make my mascot comeback. I haven't figured out how yet. But I will.

8
Don't Go Bacon My Heart

Something's seriously off on Monday.

When I walk into first-period math, a strange hush falls over the room. I sit in my seat in the front row and get that heavy feeling like when people stare at you from behind.

In second-period Spanish, the girl behind me whispers into her friend's ear, and I swear I hear her say my name. I swear.

Then, in computer science, I'm minding my own business, searching for platypus images, when Cole, Duke's friend who I hardly ever talk to, squeaks his chair next to mine.

"Yo, Ben." He nods at me, his wavy hair flopping around the top of his head. "Anything interesting happen to you lately?"

He knows.

"Um, no?" I say. Deny, deny, deny.

He tosses his buddy a knowing look and quickly says, "Never mind."

Seriously, what is going on? If people know I'm the Spud, why don't they just come out and say it? Why all the secrecy?

The lunch bell rings, and I dash out the door. I need to get to the cafeteria to talk to Ellie. If there's a rumor going around about me, she'll know for sure. She overhears a lot of school gossip while she's reading during class.

I squeeze into a group of students flowing toward the cafeteria like a migrating school of tuna. To my left, I spot a folded piece of paper duct-taped to a locker.

My locker.

The mob pushes me forward, but I reverse direction and fight my way upstream. I have to get to that note! Has someone discovered my secret? Is it a blackmail note? A threat? *This* must be why everyone's acting so weird!

I squeeze myself out of the lunch-bound throng and stumble to my locker. I snatch the note and open it so fast the corner rips.

Ben—

I will ask you to the Winter Dance when pigs fly.

—Jayla

My heart stops beating. I review the words to make sure I read correctly.

When pigs fly, aka, never. This cannot seriously be happening.

My ears are on fire. Everyone must know about this, which is why they were acting so weird. I just got dissed by the most popular girl at school. I'll never, ever, in a million years recover.

It doesn't even make sense. Why would Jayla assume I expected her to ask me? Is she a secret mind reader? Maybe Hunter said something, the loudmouth. And it probably didn't help that I stood her up at the game last night.

But still! To send me a note like this is just not fair. I slam my palm against the locker, the fire from my ears creeping down the back of my neck and turning me into a human volcano. Jayla seemed so nice when she talked to me on Friday. Maybe she found out I was the potato. Maybe it was too dorky for her to handle. Maybe it's time

I beg my parents to let us move back to California. I officially hate it here.

The numbers on my combination dial blur together, and it takes me three tries to get the code right. I can't believe I was dumb enough to believe Jayla liked me in the first place. I'll never get my hopes up over a girl again. For as long as I live.

I crank open my locker and gasp. Three bright pink helium balloons pop out of the locker and float up to the ceiling. In thick black Sharpie, someone has scribbled pointy ears, googly eyes, and a pig snout onto each balloon.

Ohhhhh. *I will ask you to the Winter Dance when pigs fly.*

The realization smacks a smile onto my face. This isn't a dis. This is just one of those creative ways girls ask guys to dances. My whole body sighs in relief, like I just woke from a nightmare to realize I'm safe in bed. No one knows I'm an undercover potato. Everything will be all right.

All right? Better than all right! Jayla Marden asked me to the dance. *Me.* I've heard of people pinching themselves to make sure they're not dreaming, but I've never understood the feeling until today.

I check out the contents of my locker to make sure I didn't leave anything embarrassing in there, like a stinky pair of gym socks or a half-eaten sandwich. I'm safe this time, but I'll have to be more careful in the future. How'd Jayla get my locker code anyway?

Who cares? I'm going to the dance with the most beautiful girl at South Fork Middle School.

Looks like Idaho Ben is gonna have to get better at talking to girls.

• • •

I burst through the cafeteria doors in a daze and breathe in the trademark scent of grease, pizza sauce, and sweaty armpits. It's a wonderful day to be alive!

The pizza line is too long, so I get some chicken nuggets and hurry to my table. I weave around groups of students, dodge a poorly placed trash bin, and pass a few basketball players reaching up the bottom of the vending machine to try to steal some chips.

I hop over the table bench and plop down next to Ellie.

"Somebody looks chipper today," she says. "Got good news?"

"You could say that." I tell her and Hunter about Jayla's note and the pigs, making sure to skip the part, of course, where I mentally accused Hunter of being a loudmouth. Turns out Ellie overheard during her first period that I'd gotten asked. It feels weird but flattering to be the source of other people's conversations.

After hearing about the balloon pigs, Hunter places his hand over his heart. "That's adorable. Just adorable. I am touched."

"I'm happy for you too, Ben." Ellie pulls a Tupperware out of her lunch bag. "How are you gonna answer her?"

I frown. "Can't I just say yes?"

"No. You can definitely not just say yes." She peels the lid off her Tupperware to reveal cubes of cantaloupe. "Jayla asked creatively; you answer creatively. That's how it works."

"Oh, I know!" Hunter says. "Do something that has to do with pigs. Like, spell out 'yes' in bacon or something. That would be creative. And delicious."

"Yeah, maybe. I'll think about it." It's not the worst idea. At least I'd get to eat the extra bacon.

"If I got asked," Hunter says, "that's how I'd answer, even if they didn't ask me with pigs. Because bacon is a gift of love."

Ellie wiggles her eyebrows at him. "Well, you just might get to use that answer. Lucy said some interesting things about you over the weekend."

I swallow my last chicken nugget. "Who's Lucy?"

"What'd she say?" Hunter asks at the same time.

Ellie answers me first. "She's a friend I brought to the game on Friday. We know each other from history class."

It must have been that girl I saw Hunter flexing at in the stands. "The one with curly hair?"

Ellie tilts her head. "You know her?"

Shoot. I wasn't supposed to have seen her. "Um, no. I mean, yeah—"

"Tell me! What did she say?" Hunter interrupts, saving me from a forced explanation.

"She said"—Ellie pauses dramatically—"that you were cute."

"*Cute?* No!" He slams his fist on the table.

Ellie gives him the side-eye. "Hunter, you're overreacting."

"But I hear how my sisters talk! 'Cute' is for puppy dogs! And boys you plan on dumping into the friend zone! Ben, am I overreacting?"

"Of course not." I smirk. "She probably hates you."

He sighs. "I guess it wasn't meant to be."

"Hunter." Ellie raises her spork. "If Lucy asks you to the dance, and you reject her because she called you *cute,* I will personally"—she stumbles—"do something very bad. To you."

"Stab him with your spork?" I suggest.

Hunter laughs and grabs a piece of her cantaloupe. "You know I'm just playing. I'd be stoked if she asked me. Although, there is one thing that makes me nervous."

"Oh, great," says Ellie.

"I think she's a cat person."

"What's wrong with being a cat person?" Ellie says. "I like cats."

"Yes," he explains, "but you also like dogs. Therefore, I would not classify you as a true cat person. Cat people worship their cats above all else."

"I had a neighbor who was a cat person." I point to the scar above my left eyebrow. "Her precious kitty Tater Tot gave me this."

"Don't encourage him," Ellie says. "I'm sure Lucy doesn't worship cats."

Hunter bounces on the bench. "Oh yeah? She's got a picture of her cat in her locker. That's literally the definition of idol worship if you ask Aunt Susan."

"Don't you have a poster of a horse in your room?" Ellie asks.

"That's different! If Lucy were a horse person, that'd be awesome!"

"That's so hypocritical!"

"Okay," I say, hoping to abandon the subject before a full-on fight breaks out. "Let's say Hunter gets asked to the dance by the cat worshipper. Assuming he doesn't scare her off by trying to convert her to his horse religion, he'll go with Lucy. I'm going with Jayla. That leaves you, Ellie."

"Well, I'm not gonna ask anyone," Ellie says firmly.

"Why not?" I nab a piece of cantaloupe. Six chicken nuggets were not enough to fill me up.

She shrugs. "There's no one to ask."

"There are plenty of fish in the sea!" Hunter sweeps his arm across the room. "Just look at all the fish in this cafeteria! The real problem—and if you search deep, deep down, you know it's true: You're. Too. Picky."

"Am not!" She sees me coming in for her last piece of cantaloupe and pops it in her mouth. "Honestly," she says after swallowing, "I have no desire to go to this dance. But if I had to ask someone, it would probably be Cole."

"Cole?" I say. "Really?" Over at the basketball table, Cole from computer science mixes together a smoothie of milk, ketchup, and salad dressing. Those basketball guys are always having all the fun.

"What's wrong?" Ellie says. "You don't like him?"

"Huh? I like him." But something in my stomach doesn't believe my own words, so I backtrack. "I just don't think he seems like your type."

"Why not?"

"I don't know. I just don't think you'd mesh."

Ellie shoots me a dirty look. "What is my type, then, according to you?"

"I don't know, maybe someone more studious? Like . . . Eric Daniels." Eric's this genius dude who carries around a Rubik's Cube like it's his stuffed animal. He always wears dress shirts, which is kind of weird, but he seems like a nice guy.

Now Ellie's glaring at me. I honestly don't get what I said wrong.

I glance at Cole again. He pumps his fist as Duke chugs the ketchup smoothie. I notice Cole's pointy chin, brown loafers, and green sweater vest. "Plus," I say, "Cole looks like a Christmas elf."

"You're such a bully."

"Am not! Just because I said Cole looks like an elf does not make me a bully. It makes me an acute observer."

"Whatever." She grabs her book off the bench and starts reading.

Hunter, who has been strangely quiet throughout this Cole discussion, motions with his chin. "Well, look who it is."

I spin around.

"Be cool, man. Don't look."

"You said look."

"I didn't mean *look* look."

Jayla and Paris have left their lunch table and are headed our way. The crowds part for them like they have an enchantment over the cafeteria. Jayla wears a soft white turtleneck that looks like it's just waiting for some kid to fling ketchup at it. Part of me wants to get up and be that shirt's bodyguard.

"What are you gonna say?" Hunter whispers.

"I don't know," I whisper back. Sweat prickles the back of my neck.

The girls stop at our table, and a few of Duke's buddies eye us curiously.

"Hey, Ben. Hey, Hunter," Jayla says. She glances at Ellie reading, and then back at me. "You got my note?"

"Yeah, that was awesome!" I say loud enough so the basketball table can hear. "I loved the pigs."

"It was adorable!" Hunter agrees. Jayla flashes a smile, but I can't tell by her expression if she thinks he's funny or dorky. As awful as it sounds, I can't help but wonder if she'd be more impressed if I were sitting at Duke's table, mixing concoctions of condiments and laughing with the guys.

I'm not sure what to say next. Maybe Jayla expects me to give her an answer about the dance right now. But Ellie said I need to answer creatively, so maybe I'm supposed to keep her in suspense. They need a guidebook for these situations.

I change the subject. "How'd you get into my locker, anyway?"

"That was me." Paris twirls the single blue streak in her dark brown hair, looking like either this is the most boring conversation in the world, or like she only got three hours of sleep. "I looked over your shoulder when you were opening your locker this morning. Wasn't too hard."

Jayla tugs on her sleeve. "She even kept watch down the hallway to make sure no one grabbed the note off your locker."

"Smart." I try not to wince. Was Paris spying on me

when I read the fake "rejection" note? I hope she didn't see my sappy facial expression.

An awkward silence follows. It's funny how you can have silence with your friends and it's no big deal, but have silence when your crush is around and it's like you're failing at being a functioning human being.

There's gotta be a way to address the dance without giving away my answer. After some thought, I say, "Well, I'm excited to answer you."

"Creatively," Hunter adds.

"Cool," Jayla says. The girls exchange a glance, as if telepathically communicating that it's time to go.

"Uh . . . see you in English, I guess," Jayla says, and they leave. Overall, I'd say that wasn't a complete disaster. Idaho Ben is getting—dare I say it?—smooth?

Once they're out of earshot, Hunter sighs. "That was a beautiful moment. You guys think Paris likes horses?"

"You're ridiculous," Ellie says, not bothering to look up from her book. "Besides, Paris is going to the dance with Duke."

Hunter frowns at the basketball table. "Well, I can't compete with him. That guy's massive."

Ellie peeps over the top of her book. "I don't get his appeal. He doesn't seem very nice. I can't stand guys who aren't nice." She emphasizes the words "aren't nice" while looking at me. I must've gotten on her bad side for insulting what's-his-elf-face. Maybe I should say something nice about him to even things out, but for some reason, I can't bring myself to do it.

I check my phone for the time. "Three minutes till the bell."

Ellie looks up. "Is it already that late?" She snaps her book shut and stuffs it under her arm. "I have to get to orchestra." She collects her things and hurries away.

My stomach growls. Apparently, the few cubes of cantaloupe weren't enough either. "Hey, Hunter, you gonna eat that salami?"

"Nah. Take it." He tosses me the half-foot-long meat stick. His mom always puts the most random stuff in his lunch bag.

I tear off the plastic wrap and take a salty bite. "Did Ellie seem mad to you?"

"Yeah." He squirms a little. "I think she likes that Cole guy. I don't know."

"Weird."

"Yeah. Weird."

What does Cole have that interests Ellie anyway? I've never even seen him talk to her. What if she asks him to the dance and he says yes? What if he becomes better friends with her than me? And invites her to eat lunch at their table?

I shake off the thought. There's no point worrying about something that will never happen. I should focus on my own date instead.

I play out the scene in my head:

SETTING: Middle school gymnasium. No bouncy house in sight. Lights are dimmed, and music begins to play.

BEN: *(taking Jayla by the hand)* Shall we dance?

JAYLA: *(a gleam in her eye)* We shall, and never stop!

BEN twirls JAYLA, her white skirt flowing around her. He dips her and lifts her back up.

I hope dipping girls is as easy as they make it look in the movies.

I take another bite of salami and head to my next class. Excitement bubbles in my chest like a shaken can of soda. Out of all the guys in the school, Jayla picked me. Walked right up to me in the cafeteria with everyone watching. I feel like I have an aura shining around my head, like I'm the Chosen One in some fantasy novel.

The Chosen One. I got it. I know how I'm gonna answer Jayla.

I have to start working on it right after school if I'm gonna pull it off.

9

The Stomach Pretzel

There's a NO EATING sign on the wall of my English classroom, so I stuff the rest of the salami in my mouth and head straight to my seat in the back corner. I have the desk right next to the air freshener plug-in, which today happens to smell like cinnamon. I'm thumbing through my notebook and thinking about my answer for Jayla, when a flash of orange catches my eye. It's Mitch entering the room in his big puffy jacket. He looks straight at me and flashes this goofy smile that seems to say, *Hey, secret buddy. LOL*. Just like that, with the cheesiness and everything. I grimace back, wondering if this kid will now expect me to publicly befriend him. I almost think he's gonna walk up to my desk and ask, *Did you think about what kind of drone you'd like?* But instead he sits in his seat like any other day.

The bell rings and Ms. Wu claps three times, which is her way of getting our attention. Her blue skirt and matching jacket remind me of a flight attendant—one of the really nice ones who gives you extra peanuts.

"All right, everyone," Ms. Wu says. "Today we're doing group work. Find a group of two or three. You have sixty seconds."

Duke points at me and then to his chest. "Partners?"

I nod and can't help but grin. Duke always used to pair up with Kevin in the third row, but apparently he thinks I'm the coolest kid in the class now.

Duke snakes his way through the rows to reach me in the back corner. He nabs an absent girl's chair, flips it around, and straddles it like it's a horse.

The rest of the students mill around the classroom and clump their desks together. Meanwhile, Mitch stays put, his head turning right and left like he's watching one of his drones fly around the room.

I feel for the guy. The phrase "find a partner" used to send me into a panic attack at my last school. Everyone always paired up so fast, each tick of the clock chipping away at my chances to find someone to work with.

Mitch taps the shoulder of the guy sitting across from him. "Hey, can I join your group?"

"Sorry, we already have three," the boy says as a girl sweeps in beside him.

I think about calling out, *Hey, Mitch, come here,* but I can just imagine the weirded-out face Duke would make. Maybe I can point out another group for him to join. I survey the room. Group of three. Group of three. Group of two! No, their third member is just sharpening his pencil.

The only groups of two left in the whole class are me and Duke, and Mikenna and Mikelle—who are not, as their names suggest, twins with cheesy parents, but rather best friends who are so exclusive that I don't think they'd let Taylor Swift herself join their group.

For Mitch, this must be like choosing between brussels sprouts and dog food, because his options are down to me and Duke, who could snap him in half if he got on his bad side, and the two girls giggling in the corner. I open my mouth, but my voice clings to the back of my throat.

Duke keeps talking to me—something about throwing oranges, I think? I "uh-huh" back without really listening, curious to see how the Mitch-needs-a-partner saga will end.

Mitch slowly stands and makes his way toward us. What is he thinking?

"Here comes Mitch the Snitch," Duke mutters. "Let's pretend we have a third partner already. Like an imaginary friend."

"Ha, okay," I say, and my stomach immediately twists itself into a pretzel.

Mitch is just a few feet away, and I can tell from his twitchy mouth that he's just as nervous as I am. This can't end well. I avert my eyes to the corner of the room. *Turn around, Mitch. Just turn around.*

"Hey!" Ms. Wu points at the group by the whiteboard, singling out two boys spitting water at each other through their teeth. "Nuh-uh. You guys are not allowed to be partners anymore." She looks around. "Peter, go join Mikenna and Mikelle. We'll have Mitch take your place."

Close call.

Mitch scoots his desk to join the water spitter and his partner, and a weight lifts off my shoulders. It's almost like Ms. Wu saw what was going on and stepped in to save the day.

This annoying voice in my head says I'm a jerk and I should've asked Mitch to sit with us. But why should I feel obligated? Just because he's the only person who knows I'm the Spud doesn't mean we're BFFs all of a sudden. We talked for like five minutes in the janitor's closet. Big deal.

Still, I can't help but feel bad about how it all went down. The nervous face he made walking up to us sticks in my brain, if that makes sense. It also doesn't help that I end up completing the "group work" all by myself, since Duke doesn't understand how to make similes. Personally, I find them as easy as pie. (See, there's one right there.) Duke might understand them too if he put in a little effort. Maybe Mitch would've made a better partner after all.

The rest of the school day goes by like ice melting on a cold day. When it ends, I rush to the bike racks to tell Ellie my idea for answering Jayla. She helps me cement the details on our walk home.

The plan is to get a plush version of Hedwig the owl, Harry Potter's pet and trusty mail carrier. I'll put a cute little envelope in her beak (that was Ellie's idea) and stuff her in Jayla's locker. I'll write something clever, playing on how Harry was the "Chosen One" in the books, and I'm her "Chosen One" to the dance.

It will be brilliant. Absolutely brilliant.

At home, I scroll through a few stuffed Hedwig options and find the biggest, fluffiest one. I buy it using Mom's credit card, which I know isn't the best choice, but in movies, parents always tell their kids they can use the credit card in case of an emergency. Mom and Dad haven't used those *exact* words, but I'm sure it's like an implied thing. And this is definitely an emergency. If I don't answer Jayla ASAP, she might change her mind.

Besides, Mom would probably let me buy the owl if I asked. I'd just rather not bring it up. If she knew it was for a girl, she'd go full-on interrogation mode: *Who's the girl? What's she like?* You get the picture.

The next day at school, I realize something that makes me want to smack my forehead: I spent so much time looking at stuffed Hedwigs that I didn't practice my mascot skills for Wednesday's game. The pressure is starting to get to me. Every time I start daydreaming about dancing with Jayla, I see myself morph into a clumsy, giant potato that knocks her to the floor. I avoid Coach in the halls, afraid he'll say something in passing like *You prepared for the game tomorrow, Hardy?* I don't want to admit that I'm not.

Last Friday, I looked Coach in the eye and promised I'd try my best. But so far, all I've done to prepare is watch YouTube videos of stunts that are either too expensive or too dangerous to pull off.

I have just one night to get my game plan down, and this time, I won't blow it.

10

Buster Almost Blows My Cover

When I get home, I remove my shoes on the front porch, like Mom always insists. I walk through the door and am hit with the sounds of a normal afternoon in the Hardy household: Mom's in the kitchen, talking to Grandma on the phone about how the renovation is coming along. Dad's in the living room, hammering a shelf to the wall. Abby's in the front room, practicing her violin. She's gotten a lot better since starting fifth grade.

"I'm home," I call out to Mom before heading upstairs. Now she won't come check for me. I'm going all out on my mascot training, and I need to be alone.

I lock myself in my room and take a deep breath. Time to buckle down.

I rummage through the books and video games on my

desk until I find a pencil and notebook, and then I belly flop onto my bed. I flip to a blank page and brainstorm.

MASCOTTING IDEAS

Moonwalk

Handstand

Start the wave

High-five people

Cooler dance moves

Juggle

This'll be good to start with.

I pull out my phone and play a fast-paced song—perfect for moonwalking inspiration. I hop off my bed and moonwalk around piles of clothes until I ram my ankle into my skateboard. My feet don't seem bendy enough. I massage them and persevere. By the end of the song, I figure I'm getting better. Hopefully, the crowds won't demand moonwalking perfection from the potato. What's next on the list?

Handstand. I do one against the wall to get a feel for it, and then I try a couple in the center of my room. I position myself in front of the beanbag for a safe landing, which comes in handy. On my third attempt, I time myself at twenty-four seconds. Not too shabby. But I'll have to practice in the actual costume to see if I can pull it off.

Next, *start the wave* and *high-five people*. I'll keep them in mind, but they require no practice.

Then, *cooler dance moves*. I really need something besides the Coach Tudy–inspired kick-punch.

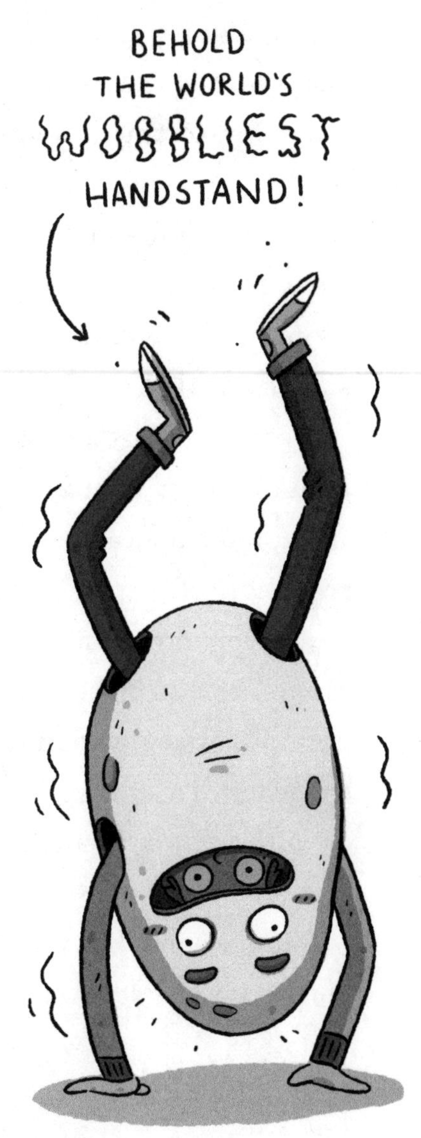

I pull up a search for "potato dancing," hoping to find some moves I can manage while dressed like a spud. Instead I discover that there's a legit dance called the Mashed Potato that was popular in the 1960s, kinda like the Twist. Apparently, it even inspired a song called "Mashed Potato Time" by Dee Dee Sharp. I couldn't make this stuff up if I tried.

A two-minute YouTube video explains how to do it. Heels together. Swing out one leg. Heels together.

Swing out the other leg. Sheesh. This is way harder than the Twist.

I check out a couple of other recommended videos. My favorite is a routine led by a giant pink otter from Japan. I don't understand the captions, but the otter is easy to follow, and she's a surprisingly good dancer. I guess mascotting is a universal language, like music, or math.

Finally I'm ready for the last item on my list: *juggle.* Now, *there's* something I can brush up on. I search my room for a juggling prop. I need something round . . . something that can fit in my hands . . . something like . . .

Potatoes! That'd be a crowd pleaser. And considering how my mom hoards potatoes like she's preparing for the zombie apocalypse, a few missing spuds will surely go unnoticed.

I creep downstairs and peek into the kitchen for Mom. She'd be pretty weirded out if she saw me carrying potatoes up to my room, and she would probably assume the worst. I'm not sure what the worst thing is you can do with potatoes, but she'd come up with some strange idea.

Mom's gone, but probably not for long, since a pot's boiling on the stove. I slink into the pantry, nab three potatoes, and glide back up the stairs, hoping Abby's too focused on her violin to notice me.

Halfway up, Buster yelps from behind me, nearly giving me away. He's muscled his way up to the third step and is struggling to make it to the fourth. His baby corgi legs can only take him so far. Genetics are not on his side.

"Poor little guy." I scoop him up and cradle him in my arms over the potatoes. I lock my door behind us and set him on my bed. He'll be my audience.

Buster nestles into my fuzzy blue sheets and watches me juggle, perking up his golden head and barking each time a potato drops to the floor.

My motions are a bit wobbly. I'm out of practice, since we don't have orange trees in our backyard anymore. Also, perfectly round oranges are easier to juggle than potatoes. But I keep at it, and I'm just starting to find my rhythm when someone knocks on my door.

"Can I come in?" my sister says. "I want to play with Buster!" Classic Abby. She just *has* to wait until I have Buster before wanting to play with him.

Saying no would be useless. Abby never gives up. I stuff the spuds under my pillow and open the door to shoo out Buster, but he doesn't waltz out like I planned. Instead he darts around the room, tail wagging and tongue hanging out. Abby squeezes past me and reaches for him with her skinny arms. "Buster!" she squeals.

Buster was our parents' consolation gift to us when we moved to Idaho. Like, *Sorry for uprooting you kids and destroying your childhood stability. Here's a puppy.* I was pretty upset about leaving behind the beach and the sun and the skate parks, but getting Buster definitely helped me cope. A puppy can soften nearly all of life's problems.

Buster starts to wear himself out, so I put him on my pillow to rest. Abby plunks herself on my bed beside him, causing a potato to roll out from its hiding place.

Nooooooo! I mentally scream. Seriously, what's wrong with me? I can't even manage to successfully hide a *potato.*

Abby lifts my pillow to reveal the other fugitive spuds. She scrunches up her freckly nose like she smells a stinky old sneaker. "Why are there potatoes under your pillow?"

This is bad. This is really bad. If Abby suspects anything, she'll snoop around until she discovers what's going on. She's got a future as a spy, I swear. She figures out what Mom and Dad are going to get her every single Christmas.

"It's a science experiment," I say.

"Huh?"

"I'm"—I clear my throat—"you know, studying the effects of sleep deprivation on the human brain. The lumps under the pillow make it hard to sleep."

She eyes me suspiciously, giving herself a double chin. "Is that really the kind of stuff you do in middle school?"

"What, scientific studies? Of course." I toss a potato casually in the air.

"Riiight," she says, in a way that leaves me unsettled. Abby's a bigger blabbermouth than Hunter. If she ever finds out I'm the Spud, she'll tell Mom and then her friends. I'll never hear the end of it.

Abby makes herself comfy on my bed, which tells me she's not planning on leaving anytime soon. I prepare to guard myself against fierce questioning.

"So, you heard me playing the violin, right?" She tucks her dark blond hair behind her ear. "What did you think?"

My body relaxes. I am more than happy to abandon the potato conversation.

I sit next to her on the bed and wink. "I think I need to invest in some noise-canceling headphones." Abby's talented, but she's been practicing so much lately that even Mom has suggested she play in the garage. One can only handle so many renditions of "When the Saints Go Marching In."

Abby pouts. She clearly didn't think my joke was funny.

"Come on." I nudge her shoulder. "It's just . . . I don't know. Maybe you should play some different songs every now and then."

Abby buries her head in my pillow and screams something indecipherable. Note to self: Wash that pillowcase.

"You okay?" I ask.

She finishes off a couple of short screaming bursts into the pillow and then calmly lifts her head. "Well, you'll be happy to know I'm quitting the violin."

I shake my head. "You know I was just kidding. Don't quit because I'm a jerk."

"It's not because of that." She falls back into my mattress. "I'm just not good anymore."

"You sound good to me."

"No, I don't. I stink! No matter how hard I practice for the chair tests, I can't get past the third stand. The *third stand*! Do you know how humiliating that is?" She flings herself off the bed and face-flops onto the beanbag.

"You'll do better next time," I say. "It's not that big a deal." If only the most embarrassing thing I had to worry about were a seat in an orchestra.

"You don't understand," she says. "Back in LA, I was the best in the whole class. Now I know that I was only good because everyone at Wilson stank."

"They didn't stink."

"Yes, they did. You should see the people here. Brielle Mendoza is first chair. She started violin lessons when she was six, and she's already playing 'Orange Blossom Special.' I'll never beat that."

I'm not sure what to say. I guess it would be hard to feel like no matter how much you practiced, it didn't make a difference. What if after all my mascot training, I still blow it tomorrow?

At least I'll do better than if I never practiced at all.

I pick up a potato and dig at it with my fingernail. "Maybe the competition is good for you. Even if you're not better than Brielle, you're better than you used to be."

"I guess."

"Brielle's helping you, in a way. If you'd stayed at Wilson, you wouldn't have tried as hard."

"True."

I shrug. "Who knows? Moving here might've been the best thing that ever happened to your musical career."

"Musical career?" She giggles. "I'm ten years old, you weirdo."

"I can see the headlines now: 'Abby Hardy, classical violinist—' "

"I want to fiddle!"

"Okay, okay. 'World-famous fiddler! Performing at—' "

"Disneyland!"

"The happiest place on Earth."

She sighs, sinking into the beanbag. "I still miss being the best."

I laugh. Abby's so competitive. I'd like to get her and Hunter's sisters together for a game of Uno and see who survives.

Ding!

The doorbell rings. A few seconds later, Mom's voice drifts up the stairs. "Did somebody order a package?"

My package for Jayla! Oh, blessed next-day shipping! "Whoa," says Abby as I drop the potato and dash out the bedroom door. I gallop downstairs and rip open the box right in the entryway. It looks just like Hedwig, down to the dark spots on her snowy-white wings. It's perfect. I'll answer Jayla tomorrow.

Mom clears her throat behind me, and I slowly turn around.

"Why'd you order an owl?" She squints, hands on her hips. "You better not have used my credit card."

Busted. I should've waited outside for the delivery truck. Or pretended I had no clue where the package came from and then convinced Mom to let me keep it anyway. So many rookie mistakes.

"Benjamin," Mom says in a tone that could freeze water. "Explain."

There's one surefire way I can escape punishment. But is it *really* worth it?

"I . . ." I check to make sure Abby didn't follow me down, and then I whisper, "I bought it for a girl."

It works. Mom's eyes light up, and then her anger transforms into intense curiosity. "A girl? What's her name?"

"Jayla."

"Is she in your classes?"

"Yes."

"What's she like?"

"Moooooom."

"Is she your girlfriend?"

"No! It's just for a dance. It's not a big deal."

Abby yells from upstairs, "A *dance*?"

Oh brother.

Abby joins us, and she and Mom ooh and aah over the owl's fluffiness. Part of me wants to go hide in the closet and not come out until they go to bed.

At least they help me work on my answer. Mom digs some scarlet and gold ribbon out of her craft box, and Abby helps with the wording of the letter. It's nice that they care, but they definitely tend to overdo things. They'll probably expect me to give a full play-by-play of Jayla's reaction tomorrow.

This owl better be worth it.

11

All That and a Bag of Chips

There's nothing as tense as the last sixty seconds of the school day. Everyone grips their binder and perches on the edge of their seat like an Olympian runner waiting for the gunshot.

But when the final bell rings on Wednesday, I calmly pack my binder. I even throw in a "Thanks for the lesson" to my history teacher, Mr. Ziegler, just for kicks. Today I'm in no rush.

I loiter outside the classroom door, occasionally peeking around the corner to watch the lockers. Still no sign of Jayla. Any minute now.

My answer to the dance is all set up in Jayla's locker, and I want to see her reaction. Earlier today I found Paris in the halls and asked if she could do some locker-code sleuthing for me. "You want Jayla's combo?" She winked and smacked her gum. "It's ten-eighteen-two." Either Paris has a weird obsession with finding out everyone's locker code, or that's just the type of thing girls tell each other.

Then, during history, I "went to the bathroom." I had to ask like three times since Mr. Ziegler annoyingly didn't believe I needed to go. Once he caved, I grabbed the items from my locker, opened Jayla's locker, and set everything up.

Jayla's voice comes from around the corner. I spy from down the hall as she approaches her locker with Paris, enters her code, and cranks open the door. Crammed into the locker is the giant stuffed Hedwig.

Jayla gasps. "Aww! It's so cute!"

"Oh, no fair!" Paris says.

Jayla wrestles Hedwig out of the locker, and the note taped to her beak drops to the floor. Jayla picks it up and reads: " 'Jayla, I'm glad to be your "Chosen One." Can't wait to go to the dance with you.' "

"How sweet," Paris says with a tinge of jealousy in her voice. "Duke answered *me* by throwing me a paper airplane during math class that said, 'Yes.' "

Everything's going as planned. Next I'll go up and surprise her. I sweep my hands through my hair and turn the corner.

"It's random he got me an owl, though," Jayla says.

I stop in my tracks.

She reexamines the note. "Nothing in the note says anything about an owl. I thought people usually answered with a pun, or something clever."

"Yeah," Paris agrees. "Maybe he just likes owls."

I blink. Did I hear correctly? Come on, Jayla, the note says I'm the "Chosen One"! Like Harry! That's Hedwig the owl! I even burned the corners of the letter to make it look old and drew a lightning scar at the top. Have I entered some alternate universe where J. K. Rowling was never born?

I have to get out of here before they catch me spying. I creep back to the corner.

And then I sneeze. Because sneezes insist on coming at the worst times.

"Ben, is that you?" Jayla pokes her head out from behind Hedwig.

"Oh hey." I reluctantly walk up to them. "Uh, so, you like the owl?"

She hugs it tight to her chest. "I love it!"

I cough. "It's Hedwig, by the way. You know, from Harry Potter."

"Oh right," she says with a confused look on her face.

"Harry Potter's for nerds!" pipes up Paris. Not eager to get on my good side, this one.

"Guess I'm a nerd," I say with a grin, unable to think of a witty comeback on the spot. I should've said something clever like *You must be a Slytherin*, but she caught me off guard.

"I think Harry Potter's kind of cool," says Jayla, but her tone doesn't have me convinced. "I saw a couple of those movies."

I almost dive into my classic rant about how the movies can't compare with the books, but considering my audience, it wouldn't be worth it.

I say that I'll see them later and then pass the bike racks before heading home, in case Ellie's waiting for me. No luck. During sixth period I texted her to wait up, but I probably took too long to show. Or maybe she's annoyed that I still haven't bought that game-day shirt she keeps bugging me about. Or maybe she doesn't care about walking home with me anymore. That last option bothers me the most of all.

I walk home alone and, two hours later, return for the basketball game. I reenact Operation: Mascot Transformation, determined to make it go more smoothly this time around. When I get to the janitor's closet, I set aside the surrounding mops and brooms before dressing, so I won't knock them over. Then I take out the Febreze I brought from home and spray it inside the headpiece.

Now it smells like tropical mist (on a potato-farming island, granted, but at least it's an improvement). And then there's my most brilliant idea yet: a mini portable fan. I found it in the basement in one of our unpacked junk boxes. But it is junk no more. This baby will save me from drowning in a lake of my own sweat. I turn it on and duct-tape it to the inside of the helmet. The breeze feels almost like a day at the beach. Perfect.

Before the game, I stand at the entryway to the gym and hold my hand up to every single person who comes in. If they don't high-five me, I go ahead and high-five their stubborn little arms, with an occasional high five to the face for the particularly dismissive ones.

Maybe I've just been sniffing so much Febreze that my brain has stopped functioning correctly, but being a mascot suddenly doesn't seem so bad. The mesh screen in front of my eyes is like magic. I can see people who can't see me back. I stand two feet in front of people from my classes, and they have no idea it's me slapping their hand, or their arm, or their face. I'm like a fly on the wall, except with no buzzing and, hopefully, a longer life span.

Tonight we're playing the Alta Heights Fire Ants, a team we're expected to beat. Not many people show up—maybe fifty tops, half the crowd of last Friday. Not everyone has as much school spirit as Wyatt, the ex-mascot. He waves his crutches from the front row with a smile so big that the gleam off his braces could blind the players.

Unlike Hamilton, Alta Heights is a school no one thinks much about. They have nothing to admire and nothing to hate, kind of like vanilla yogurt. And get this—they don't even have a mascot! That's how lukewarm they are about their sports teams.

The tinny whistle calls the teams to center court for the jump ball, and the game is on. Instead of retreating to my wooden bench, I walk up the bleachers and sit next to a mom, dad, and son like I just happen to be a part of their family. The kid, who's probably four years old, gawks at me as if I'm Santa Claus himself.

He tugs his mom's sleeve. "Mom, look at that!"

The woman eyes me suspiciously, like I'm a kidnapper in disguise. "Looks like the Spud wanted to sit by you."

The boy pokes a finger into my suit. "I like him, Mom."

I laugh and ruffle the kid's hair. It's nice to see I've already made a fan.

Our team is off to a great start, but the applause is polite and pathetic. It's like the crowd thinks they're watching golf instead of basketball.

Coach would want me to bring out some energy.

Didn't he say "mascot" means "lucky charm" in French? Or was it German? Either way, I better get up and lucky-charm the heck out of this place.

Mascots have no shame, I repeat to myself, and then I stand on the bench and cup my hand to my invisible spud ear. Amazingly, the cheers crescendo. I raise the roof, and they grow even louder. What kind of magic is this? I feel the power! I almost break out into dance, but I think it would be bad form to distract from the actual game.

Near the end of the first quarter, the Fire Ants call their first time-out, score 14–10, Spuds. We've stayed ahead the whole game, but only by a basket or two. If I can get some more momentum going, it might be enough to push us further ahead.

As the teams huddle on the court, I bust out the moves I practiced yesterday. I moonwalk across the floor, and the fans in the front rows clap. Then I break out my new signature move.

"He's doing the Mashed Potato!" yells an old woman in the third row. She and her husband have a good chuckle over that. They might be the only two in the whole crowd who've been alive long enough to understand the reference.

During the next time-out, I channel the energy of

Chi-tan the Otter: I slide to the left, slide to the right, crisscross my feet, and turn. I body roll, but it probably just looks like I'm convulsing. And those are all the moves I can remember.

Knowing I can't repeat myself now that people are actually watching, I resort to one of the few dances I know by heart, and one I've mastered over the years: the "Macarena." Apparently, people think a potato shaking its hips is hilarious, because when I get to the "Heyyy, Macarena" part, I get lots of laughs—and not the mean *You're a loser* laughs, but the good-natured *Would you look at that* laughs. It's all in the tone.

By halftime, we're six points ahead. Time to check another item off my Mascotting Ideas list: *start the wave.*

While the cheerleaders do their routine, I run to one end of the bleachers, crouch to the floor, and pop up with my hands above my head. The fans catch on, rising in their seats one after another as the wave ripples down the stands.

I run across the bottom of the bleachers, following the wave, and start it up again on the other side. As I turn to run back to my starting point, I notice Ellie and Hunter up in the top left corner. I tip my head back to get a better look. Ellie is wearing a nice maroon-colored shirt that I've never seen her wear before. Beside her,

Hunter hops on the bench, totally out of sync with the wave. They must have come in late, because I would've definitely face-fived them if I'd seen them walk in.

Anyway, all these thoughts pass through my head as I'm running back for the wave, and before I know it, I trip over my own feet and am diving toward the floor. Leaning my head back while running in a potato helmet was not my brightest idea.

I flop to the court and find myself bowling-ball rolling toward the cheerleaders. They're stacked on top of each other like a human deck of cards. I steamroll into the girl at the corner, and her elbows buckle, causing the whole pyramid to collapse. Down they come like bowling pins—bowling pins that can squeal, anyway.

Jayla tumbles on top of me from the second row. It might even be romantic if I weren't in a potato suit.

"Agh! Stupid potato!" she yells. I'm speechless.

Paris, the cherry on top of the cheerleader sundae, takes the hardest hit. "You klutz!" she cries out, rubbing her backside.

The crowd, meanwhile, is having a field day, hooting and hollering with gigantic grins on their faces. Some hold out their phones to record the aftermath of the spill. You'd think everyone would hate me for ruining the cheer pyramid, but apparently no one can resist a good mascot fail.

The cheerleading coach double-checks that none of the girls injured themselves, and the second half begins with high momentum. The Spuds stretch their lead, and the final buzzer rings with a score of 78–59, Spuds, a total landslide. As the fans exit, I stand near the doorway, this time not forcing high fives on everyone, but rather receiving them from my adoring fans.

"Yeah, buddy!" says a guy from my math class. He pounds my fist as he heads out.

"You rock, potato dude!" says a girl I've never met.

Man, it feels good to finally be appreciated.

Ellie and Hunter are hanging out at the bottom of the bleachers. What do they think of Mr. Spud?

It'd be too easy to go mess with them. Swing Ellie's braid or something.

I sneak up behind her, but right as I'm reaching for her hair, up walks Cole the Elf. I back off.

He wipes sweat off his forehead. "Hey, Ellie! What's up?"

"Hey!" I can tell she's smiling from her voice. "You were great tonight."

As a matter of fact, Cole was not "great." He made probably three or four baskets the whole game.

"Thanks." Cole shoves his floppy hair out of his face. "It was a good game."

So he's not even going to own up to the fact that he stank? Okay, then.

Ellie shoots me a wary glance, and I realize how weird I must look standing motionless and staring at them. I wander off to high-five a couple of girls from my science class while straining to eavesdrop.

"I didn't think I was gonna make that basket in the last quarter," Cole says. Pfft.

"Me neither," Ellie says. "You were pretty heavily guarded."

"Yeah." Cole scratches his elbow. "Well, I should probably go change." He lifts his arms and leans in for a hug. Gross. Ellie wouldn't want to be covered in all that sweat.

She hugs him back—probably just to be polite—and my stomach clenches. Now she'll smell like his nasty BO.

Ellie lets go first. "See you in math!"

"Yeah, for sure!"

Wait, math? No way is Cole in the upper-level math class with Ellie. She must have switched into the lower level or something. I'll ask her about it tomorrow.

Coach spots me and marches up to pat my shoulder. "Good work, son. I loved the whole knocking-over-the-cheerleaders routine." He chuckles to himself. "That really got the crowd going, didn't it?"

"You know I didn't do that on purpose, right?"

He winks. "Just play it off like you did. Nice touch starting the wave, by the way. It's not easy running in that costume. I'm proud of you for not giving up."

My face breaks out in a huge smile. Normally, I'd try to play it cool, but Coach can't see me under the headpiece anyway. I'm feeling the same warm rush I used to get after conquering the half-pipe at the skate park. Tonight wasn't perfect, but I did a heck of a lot better than last time. At least I made the fans laugh and want to high-five me back.

If I can do this well next game, maybe I won't mind if people find out who I am.

Maybe it wouldn't be so bad to be known as Spudboy after all.

12
Salami King

Once everyone leaves, I enter the dim hallway, squinting to make sure I don't ram into anything. Light from the janitor's closet spills into the hall as Mitch pulls out a monster-sized push mop that could swallow him whole.

"Hey, Mitch," I say. Now's a good chance to make up for ignoring him during class the other day.

He looks surprised. "Ben! What's up?"

I take off the headpiece. "Did you see the game?"

He shakes his head. "Nah. I never go."

"Well, you're not gonna believe this."

I let it all spill out. I tell him about the moonwalk, the Mashed Potato, the laughter, the cheers, the wave, and of course the human bowling-ball routine. I don't know why I'm telling him all this. I guess I want someone—anyone—to talk to about my personal victory, and he's my only option. Plus, Mitch turns out to be one of those people you can tell is really listening and not judging you for everything you say, or thinking you're a loser because you watched a dance tutorial led by an otter.

"And then the whole pyramid came tumbling down," I say, nearing the end of my story.

Mitch cackles so loudly I do a double take to make sure no one else is in the hall.

"And then Jayla Marden fell on top of me and called me a stupid potato," I continue.

"Well, that doesn't surprise me," he says. "I mean, it's Jayla."

I cock my head. "What's that supposed to mean?"

His smile vanishes and his eyes shift. "Oh, um, I don't know. I guess she just never struck me as very nice."

I cross my arms. "She's always been nice to me."

"Except for today, like you just said."

"That doesn't count. She didn't know who I was."

"Isn't that the point? It's always easier to be mean to someone when you don't know who's behind the mask."

I remember laughing at Wyatt tripping over the hot dog. That was before I even knew who he was. Mitch has a point, but I'm still annoyed he's insulting my date. "Well . . . well, I'm going with her to the dance, so . . ."

"Wait," he says. "I thought you were going out with Ellie."

Now it's my turn to laugh. "Why would you think that?"

He shrugs. "Guess 'cause I always see you guys together."

I laugh again, but Mitch just stares at me instead of joining in. "Well," I say after an awkward silence, "it's getting pretty late. I have to change and get home."

He shuffles his mop across the floor. "Yeah, okay."

I start to leave, but hesitate. "Do you . . . do you need help cleaning or anything?" It seems unfair he has to stay when I get to go home. It's like that awkward feeling of putting a dish in the sink while someone else is doing the dishes.

He grins with one side of his mouth. "Nah, this is my job, remember? If you helped, I'd have to pay you. You're not getting any money out of me."

I laugh. "How much left until you can get the quadcopter?"

"Probably like six more hours of work."

I wonder how many hours of work a stuffed Hedwig would cost. I suddenly feel bad I never had to find out. "How long are you going to be here? I really can help."

Mitch twirls the mop. "That's nice, but I think we're good. My dad's already sweeping up the gym, and I just need to take a quick pass around the halls." He grins evilly. "Now, if you want to take toilet-scrubbing duty next game, I wouldn't object."

"Ha! You'd have to pay me big-time for that."

He snickers and heads down the hall. "I'll see you in English."

"Yeah." My stomach gets all squirmy at the mention of the class where I refused to acknowledge him. It's admirable he's even talking to me after how I've treated him during school. I'll make sure to say hi to him tomorrow. Maybe I can start building up some good karma. I really need it.

• • •

My alarm rings at six-forty-five on Thursday morning, and I only snooze it once. I have to get to school early to talk to Ellie. I want to ask her a couple of questions that have been bothering me. Before first period, she and Hunter usually hang around the bench outside the media center. I don't usually join them there due to a condition I have called perpetual lateness.

Most days, my morning routine is to grab a handful

of cereal on my way out the door, speed-walk to school as fast as I can without looking like I need to pee, and slip into first period two seconds before the bell. I'm considering competing in the Olympic speed-walking event since I've gotten so much practice.

Today, however, I arrive at school five minutes before the bell. It's strangely calming to be here early. Ellie sits cross-legged on the bench, right under a poster that says YOU ARE WHAT YOU READ. She leafs through some sheet music, and Hunter paces nearby. Sitting isn't really his thing.

"Well, if it isn't the salami king himself!" Hunter says before I get the chance to speak.

Ellie translates. "A bunch of kids are walking around eating sticks of salami. He thinks it's because of you."

"There's one!" Hunter points to a boy leaning against a pillar. "Look what's in his hand."

I squint.

"Salami!" Hunter swivels his arm to the right. "And the dude by the band room with the red beanie?"

"Yeah?"

"Salami!"

"So?"

"So? I gave you my salami on Monday. Now everyone's eating salami. You, my friend, have single-handedly started a salami-eating trend."

"Sweet!" I'm starting trends? If California Ben could see me now! But in case I look like I'm bragging, I add, "I mean, it kind of sells itself. It's portable meat."

"Maybe if you wore the game-day shirt, that would catch on too," Ellie says. I keep forgetting to buy that thing. Oops.

"Dude, let's see what trend we can start next!" Hunter says. "Maybe we can bring back those slappy-hand toys. Know what I'm talking about?" He scans the hallways for more salami, giving me a chance to ask Ellie my first question. I take off my backpack and sit next to her on the bench.

Ellie turns to face me, and her hair swoops in front of her eyes. She tries to brush it away, but a stubborn strand stays put. I want to tuck it behind her ear or something . . . but that would be super weird.

I scratch my ear. "So, Ellie—did you get my text yesterday? I said I'd be late to the bike racks after school."

She takes care of the rogue hair herself. "Oh, I just figured you weren't gonna show, so I left. And my phone doesn't work. Want to explain, Hunter?"

"Not really," Hunter says. He points frantically into the distance. "Look, salami!"

Ellie crosses her arms. "It was the milk."

"What do you mean?" I ask.

She huffs. "When Hunter threw my phone in the trash, some milk spilled all over it, and now it's broken. I can't text or call."

Hunter crouches in front of the bench so he meets Ellie at eye level. "I'm so sorry." He places both hands over his heart. "I honestly forgot I was holding it."

Ellie faces me, not flattering Hunter with a smile. "Sorry if you waited for me, though."

"Don't be sorry. I'm sorry for you! My mom took my phone away for a week once, and it was torture. I use it to look up nine thousand questions a day, like 'Who's the star of *Ninja Piglets*?' or 'How do you make slime?' "

She laughs. "I think I'll survive. I already know how to make slime."

Hunter's face lights up. "Hey, I was gonna tell you—I hung out with Lucy after the game last night! I invited her to my house and everything!"

"Lucy as in . . ."

"As in Ellie's friend. The one who likes cats."

"Oh, right. Nice." I slap his hand. "How was it?"

"Incredible! I showed her the horses, and then we played Jenga."

"Jenga?" I ask. "Like the game where you pull out the—"

"The little wooden blocks, yeah." He mimes a Jenga pull. "I rock at that game!"

"It's true," Ellie says. "I've only beaten him once."

The five-minute bell echoes through the halls. Ellie stands to leave. Would it be weird to ask her my other question?

My curiosity wins.

"Hey," I say. "Did you switch into the lower-level math class?"

She adjusts her side bag. "No. Why?"

"Oh. There was just this person and he said he was in your math and . . . you know, never mind."

I'm giving myself away. I have to get out of here. But

is it true, then, that Cole's in her advanced class? There's gotta be a mistake.

"Who said they were in my math?" She narrows her eyes. "What are you talking about?"

"I'm gonna be late for class," I blurt, and book it without answering. I'll have to be more careful with what I say from now on.

13
The Invitation

It's impossible to focus in math. Daydreams are much more interesting than geometry—and, likely, just as important. Who's to say I won't become famous off one of these mental movie masterpieces?

Here's what I've got so far:

AN UNEXPECTED HERO

Written and Directed by Ben Hardy

SETTING: Grocery store checkout line. JAYLA waits patiently as CASHIER rings up her food. Suddenly ROBBER, dressed in black, barges through the front door.

ROBBER: *(waving baseball bat at cashier)* Give me all your money!

CASHIER: *(panic in her eyes)* Please, sir, put the bat down. I'll get what you want.

CASHIER rummages through cash box as JAYLA backs away in fear. Meanwhile, BEN emerges from the next aisle over, looking quite muscular in a white V-neck.

BEN: Not on my watch!

BEN snatches an abandoned cart and shoves it at ROBBER. ROBBER flips backward into cart and rolls away.

ROBBER: *(legs dangling in the air)* Gahhh!

Cart rams into tower of soup cans.

ROBBER tumbles onto the floor, buried in soup!

JAYLA: *(rushing to Ben with open arms)* My hero!

"Ben!"

"Huh?" I snap out of my daydream to see my math teacher, Ms. Meyers, hovering over my desk. As always, she looks like her bun is stretching her face out a little too tight.

I've had trouble concentrating all period. Earlier in the halls before class, Jayla walked up to me and asked for my phone number. Five minutes later she texted me a smiley emoji and a peace sign. I can't believe things are getting so serious.

"I *said,* could you please remind the class what the Pythagorean theorem is?" Ms. Meyers says.

"Oh, uh, yeah. It's like, when you have the triangle thingy and the side thingy and the thing thingy." I don't feel like thinking of math terms today.

The class chuckles, but Ms. Meyers glares.

"Sorry." I straighten my spine and force myself to focus. "A squared plus B squared equals C squared."

"That's right."

• • •

After school, I sneak into the empty gym to try my handstand in the potato suit. We have a game next Tuesday, and I gotta top my performance from last night. Coach will be counting on it.

I feel more balanced than usual as I walk across the court. Turns out, walking in a potato suit is an acquired skill, just like anything else.

It'll be easiest to do the handstand against the wall to start. I find a spot next to the bleachers and attempt to bend over, but my hands won't reach the floor. I need a running start.

I back up a few feet, run at the wall, and dive forward. My potato head hits the floor, and my feet flop up in the air. I wobble against the wall for a few seconds before crashing down.

This isn't gonna work. If I don't wanna break my neck, my feet need to stay firmly rooted on the floor. Or slightly above it . . .

An idea hits me. It's genius! How did I not think of it before? It would require a lot of work, but, if I pull it off, it'd be the most epic superstunt South Fork Middle has ever seen.

I gotta get home and start practicing right away.

• • •

The next day, I forget to bring my superstunt prop to school. I really need to practice in the gym, since half the challenge will be my execution in the suit. I'll have to go home after school to grab my stuff and then come back to train.

At least I'll get to walk home with Ellie for the first time in three days.

I meet up with her by the bike racks and we head out. It's freezing, and that's saying something when you live in Idaho. It's the kind of cold that burns your eyes, seeps through your boots, and turns your fingers into stiff, frozen sausages attached to your palms. Walking home always feels less cold, though, when I have someone to talk to, like the vibration of my vocal cords can warm up my body.

Halfway home, I tell Ellie how Mitch—who, it turns out, is in her Sunday-school class—thought we were going out. She laughs so hard that she slips on some ice. I grab her arm to steady her and slip too, nearly dragging her down. After a few heart-stopping, arm-flinging seconds, I find my balance. "You okay?" I ask, short of breath.

She laughs and clutches her chest. “What were you trying to do? Kill me?”

“Yes. I specialize in murder by ice slippage.”

She stuffs her hands in the pockets of her blue coat. “So, you talk to Mitch now?”

“Yeah, why?” The suspicious expression on her face is making me nervous.

“Oh, I just didn’t . . .” She pauses. “Didn’t think you’d talk to him, is all.”

“Why not?”

“I don’t know. He’s . . .”

I can guess what she’s thinking. “Weird?”

“Not what I was gonna say.” She tilts her head. “I mean, I guess everyone’s weird. Some people are just better at hiding it than others.”

“So what you’re saying is I wouldn’t talk to the weird kid. You think I’m too stuck-up.”

“Noooo.” She bumps into my arm. “Don’t get so offended.”

“You know,” I say, wanting to disprove her impression of me, “Mitch is a really cool guy. He actually reminds me a little of how I was at my old school.”

Ellie bundles up her face in her woolly yellow scarf, so her words come out muffled. “How so?”

I suck in the cold air, wondering if my little confession will impress her. "Like, I don't know. I was different then. I didn't have a ton of friends. I was kinda quiet."

Her lips pop out above her scarf. "You? Quiet?"

"Yeah, I know. Shocking. It's kind of embarrassing."

"Why? It's not a big deal." Ellie's gloved hand clinks against the chain-link fence we're passing. "I mean, you see how I am in Spanish. I don't talk much. So what?"

"Yeah, but that's because you're busy reading or something. I would always just sit there feeling awkward."

"Why didn't you speak up?"

"I don't know. It would've been weird."

"Why?"

I bite my cheek. "It's hard to explain. It's like, at the beginning of the school year everyone decides who's who for the rest of the year. Who's gonna be the quiet kid. Who's gonna be the funny kid. Who's gonna be the teacher's pet."

Ellie looks like she's trying to understand.

"If you try to break out of your label, it just feels weird. When I moved to Idaho, I knew I couldn't get stuck being the quiet kid again. No one at my last school even knew who I was."

"Well, your plan worked. I mean, you single-handedly

started a salami-eating trend. People definitely know who you are."

Do they, though? Because it still feels like no one knows who I really am. Not even Ellie.

I'm not the salami king. I'm the dork behind the potato mask.

We walk in silence as we pass three blobby snow figures sitting in a neighbor's front yard. It hasn't warmed up enough for them to melt completely, but just enough for them to morph into stumpy little Jabba the Hutts.

"Before I forget," Ellie says as we approach her house, "starting next week, I can't walk home on Wednesdays and Fridays anymore. I signed up to be a peer tutor."

I nudge her shoulder. "Perfect Miss Ellie."

She nudges me back. "What? It'll be fun. You should do it too."

"I don't know. . . ." I trail off. "I'm not great at math."

"People bring in all kinds of assignments. Remember how you helped me write my thesis statement? You'd be really helpful in English."

I smile. "Thanks. I guess I wouldn't mind helping people write papers and stuff."

The final basketball game's a week from today. I'll

need to use my time after school to practice my tricks. "I can't start until next week is over, though."

Ellie frowns. "Why? You have something else going on?"

"I'm grounded till next Friday, remember?" Smooth as butter.

"Your mom wouldn't even let you *tutor*?"

"Nope." I rub my hands together to heat them up. "She takes grounding very seriously. She's like a prison warden."

"Come on," Ellie says. "Your mom's super nice. She's probably like my favorite non-relative adult."

"Oh yeah? Why's that?"

"She gave me her basil plant, remember? That was so cool."

I laugh. That happened a couple of weeks ago. After walking home, I invited Ellie inside to meet Buster really quick. Mom had been in the kitchen making pasta, and Ellie was admiring her mini herb garden on the windowsill. I don't think I've ever seen anyone get so excited over plants.

"What do you do with basil anyway?" I ask.

She shrugs. "I cook with it sometimes. Or I smell it and feel pure joy."

I smirk. "Pure joy?"

"The purest of joys! Haven't you ever smelled fresh basil?"

"Can't say that I have."

"It's a sad life you lead."

We stop in front of her house, the only yellow one on the street. Icicle lights dangle from the roof, left over from Christmas. Ellie's family has a tradition to keep their decorations up until February first. Even the blue Mini Cooper in their driveway still sports reindeer antlers and a poofy red nose.

Ellie steps a few times on a crunchy pile of snow. "So I was going to invite you and Hunter to my cello recital tomorrow. I know you're grounded, but I thought I'd ask anyway. But if your mom won't even let you tutor—"

"Oh well, you never know," I cut in. "I can try to convince her. If she says no, I'll just sneak out or something."

She perks up. "You'd really do that?"

She looks impressed, so my dumb mouth keeps spewing out words. "Well, yeah. I've always wanted to hear you play. Sneaking out shouldn't be too hard. I'll pretend I'm taking a nap, do the whole pillows-under-the-covers thing, climb out the window and down the tree. It's not like this is my first rodeo." Actually, this *would* be my first rodeo if I did have to sneak out.

Ellie tells me how to get to the recital venue—an old

church building a few blocks away. I save the directions in my phone while expressing my deep appreciation for the cello and how it's my favorite instrument. I've never really thought about what my favorite instrument was until just now, but it might as well be the cello. It's in a couple of music videos I like.

Ellie walks up the concrete pathway to her door. I watch at the gate, prepared to rescue her if she slips on ice again. Once she makes it inside, I walk home with a bounce in my step. This weekend I have no homework, no basketball games, and Ellie's recital to attend. What could go wrong?

Doug Comes Back to Haunt Me

On Saturday, I wake to the worst commercial jingle ever invented.

I'M A JIGGLY JELL-O MAN
YOU'RE A JIGGLY JELL-O FAN
JIGGLY JIGGLY JELL-O IN YOUR TUM

I smack my phone off my nightstand and moan. "Ugh, Hunter."

One of Hunter's favorite hobbies is stealing my phone and changing my text alerts to annoying songs. Somehow he always manages to find a song that's more annoying than the last. It started with "Call Me Maybe." Then "Barbie Girl." Last week, "Who Let the Dogs Out" went off during math. It turned out okay, because the whole class joined in. They sang so loud, Ms. Meyers never found out it was my phone. One of my top-ten moments of the year.

I rub my eyes and open the text message from Jayla Marden: Hey Ben!

My heart skips in my chest. I answer right away.

Me: Hey! What's up?

Jayla Marden: Nothing much. I'm bored. Kind of feeling like ice cream.

I stare at the message, baffled. She wants ice cream at 9:32 in the morning? Does she want me to go get her some? Or is she just stating a random fact?

It'd be best to respond with something safe. A foolproof answer.

Me: Me too.

Jayla Marden: Haha

Why is she laughing? Girls are so confusing.

Jayla Marden: Wanna meet up later today? How about Sammy's on Tate St?

I can't believe it. She wants to see me *outside* school. My heart pounds like I just ran the mile. The idea sounds great on the surface, but it can only end in disaster. Need I recall the mistakes of my past? I'm a nonsense-spewing, water-spilling, phone-dropping fool around girls I like. The whole fantasy I've built up in my head could come crashing down the moment I say something dumb.

But Idaho Ben is not afraid of girls.

Me: Sure.

I don't want to look too eager, after all.

We decide to meet up at one-thirty p.m., which is perfect since Ellie's recital starts at noon. I can bike straight from the recital to Sammy's.

After breakfast and a shower, I put on my nicest button-down shirt and dark jeans. I have some time to kill, so I do a few handstands. Maybe I'll be brave enough to attempt one at the next game.

Before I know it, it's time to leave. On my way out the door, I realize I forgot something important. I dash back to my room and dig some bills out of the envelope on my dresser—leftover Christmas money from Grandma Hardy. I can't believe I almost forgot to bring money. Jayla would've had to pay for me. Disaster averted.

Luckily, last night's snow has melted off the sidewalks, so I'm able to ride my bike without breaking any bones. The church is a few blocks farther than I planned for. I slip into the recital room two minutes late with sore legs from having pedaled so fast.

Ellie, first on the program, faces an audience of thirty or so. Her hair is curled, which is unusual for her, but it looks really pretty. She smooths the fabric of her dark green dress and grasps the neck of her cello as I sneak into the back row. Then she begins to play.

The first note is loud. It slices through the air and hangs there for a bit. Next comes the melody. It's soft at first, so soft you have to lean forward to hear. But then it gets louder and pulls back, louder and pulls back, kind of like an ocean wave that drowns out all your other thoughts. Ellie's bow floats across the strings, and her fingers do that cool shaking thing to make the music sound like an opera lady's voice. It's beautiful. Even the little kids climbing on the stacked chairs in the back of the room stop to listen.

A few violinists follow, and then a giant cello thing called a bass, and then a viola, which is basically just a violin without the "in" at the end. They're all right, but only Ellie's playing could actually raise the hairs on your arms.

The final performer hits his last note, and everyone applauds. I hurry to congratulate Ellie, but she's surrounded by a group of people who apparently also want to tell her how talented she is. "Thank you, Tía," I hear her say to a woman in a purple sweater. "I'm glad you could make it."

I don't want to interrupt Ellie's time with family, so I

wait by the cookie table at the back of the room. There are homemade brownies, sugar cookies, and snicker-doodles galore. I bite into a gooey brownie, and it's like an explosion of sugary awesomeness. I fight the urge to stash ten of them in my jacket.

Hunter is stuck having a conversation in the front row with an old guy carrying a cane—probably a relative, since I know Hunter and Ellie have like a billion family members who live in town. The man rattles on as Hunter steals longing glances at the cookie table.

"Ben!" Ellie attacks me with a hug, and I stiffen with surprise. We've never really been *hugging* friends, not that I'm opposed to it.

"You were incredible!" I say. My hand rests on her arm a few seconds longer than is probably normal. "I literally got chills."

"Thanks." She shakes her curls out of her face. "Did you have to sneak out?"

I pull my hand back and cover my mouth to cough. "Yeah, my mom went to the mall, and she always spends like a billion hours there, so . . ."

For some reason, I feel extra bad about lying after having listened to classical music, like it activated the conscience center in my brain.

Hunter finally escapes the conversation with the

senior-citizen-slash-possible-relative. He grabs one cookie from each of the set-out plates and balances the stack in his hand. "Ellie! That was angelic. Just angelic. Aren't you glad talent runs in the family?" He takes a cookie off the top of his stack and bites into it. "Do you guys want to do something tonight? We should watch a movie or something."

"Yeah," Ellie and I say simultaneously. She looks at me and frowns. "Oh, but you're still grounded."

My face falls. "Right." Great. All I want to do is relax and watch a movie with my friends, and the only person stopping me is myself. Being fake grounded is worse than being real grounded.

Hunter mumbles through a mouthful of snickerdoodle. "How long till you're off the hook, man?"

"Next Saturday." The third game is Tuesday, and the fourth and final game is Friday. Six more days of this madness, and I'll never have to lie again.

"I'm excited for it to finally be over," Ellie says.

"Not as excited as I am," I say. "Trust me."

I check my phone: 1:25. Jayla will be at Sammy's any minute.

"Speaking of being grounded," I say, "my mom's gonna be back from the mall soon. I should probably go."

"Yeah," says Ellie. "I hope you get back in time! I'd feel

bad if you got in trouble because of this. Text me and let me know."

"Will do," I say as I walk out the door. "It was so good to see you play, Ellie."

And it really was. She's actually kind of amazing.

• • •

I mount my bike, which luckily hasn't been stolen from the side of the church. It would've vanished in two seconds if I'd left it outside in Los Angeles.

After pedaling the short distance to the diner, I hide my bike by the dumpster behind the building, just in case.

The large store window is covered in food decals—cartoon hamburgers, ice cream, french fries. I enter, and little bells attached to the door ring above my head. The place has a fifties vibe—records on the wall, black-and-white tiled floors, jukebox in the corner, the whole deal. I nod to the girl behind the counter and sit at one of the tables.

Not three minutes later, Jayla walks in wearing this amazing red turtleneck that you could see from fifty miles away. I give her an awkward side hug, and we order ice cream at the counter—me chocolate and her vanilla.

The worker wobbles as she scoops it out, thanks to the fifties roller skates strapped to her feet. I pay for both our ice creams, which I guess makes this my first official date in Idaho, and maybe even my first date ever, if you don't count the time Missy Talbot held my hand during our first-grade field trip to the zoo.

I follow Jayla past a few full booths to one by the window. The red vinyl cushions squeak when we sit.

After a brief silence, I notice a tiny silver megaphone on her charm bracelet. "How's cheer going?"

"Good." She swirls her ice cream, creating a milkshake in her cup. "Nothing too interesting."

"Nothing at all?" You'd think getting knocked down by a human bowling ball would qualify as interesting.

She purses her lips. "Well, there was this one kinda funny thing. You know the school mascot, the potato?"

I freeze for a second, the ice cream stopping on its way to my mouth. "No. I mean, yeah. Like, I don't *know* him know him, but I know of the guy, like the concept."

The corners of her mouth tighten like she's smothering a laugh. Apparently, my blabbering is amusing.

"So, get this. Last game, he rammed right into our cheer pyramid. It was awful. We all fell down and everything."

The verb "rammed" implies it was intentional. She should have more accurately said "tripped and rolled." Still, I raise my eyebrows with concern. "I hope you didn't get hurt!"

"Nah, I'm fine. Paris kind of did. Not bad, just a bruise. Either way, that potato's a moron."

My lips twitch. "Maybe it was an accident."

"Accident or not, we're gonna get back at him."

I choke on my ice cream. "Oh yeah? How?"

"I don't know." She licks her spoon. "Duke'll figure something out."

"Duke?"

"Yeah, he's mad about the whole thing because he's, like, totally in love with Paris. They're going to the dance together, you know? He texts her all the time."

I don't care so much about this Duke gossip. I care about how, exactly, Duke is planning to "get back" at me. I heard the last guy that got on his bad side ended up with a snowball to the face. In the middle of the school hallway. Not fatal, but still, he got a black eye.

I try to look casual by leaning back in the booth. "Paris told Duke to beat up the Spud, then?"

"Nah, not that intense. Duke can't afford another suspension. Plus, we don't even know who the guy is yet. Apparently, his name is Doug."

Doug? Why would she think—*ohhhhh.* I told Wyatt my name was Doug, and it must've gotten out.

"What's wrong?" Jayla asks. "Do you know him?"

My face must be giving me away. I try to relax. "Me? No. I've never met anyone named Doug in my life. Except for this one kid in kindergarten who bit everyone."

Jayla giggles. "Well, it seems like no one knows who he is, but that's his name for sure."

"How do you know?"

"Paris got it out of the old mascot." She leans in. "Get

this—she told him she needed the new Spud's name on behalf of the student council. Said they were planning to make him a monogrammed shirt."

"Like a shirt with his name on it?"

"Yeah. I don't know how she even thinks of these things. She's like an evil genius."

"No kidding." A Slytherin indeed. If she's so sneaky, what if she's able to find out that "Doug" is me? This can't be good.

On the other side of the window, a blue Mini Cooper pulls up to the curb.

A reindeer Mini Cooper.

Ellie's mom's car!

I drop my spoon. They came to get food? Why here? Why now? Weren't there enough cookies at the church? Ellie thinks I'm at home, grounded. I need to escape.

A neon exit sign glows above the back door just a couple of tables away. I'd better make a run for it.

I slide out of the booth. "Hey, I should get going."

Jayla looks surprised. "You're not even done with your ice cream."

"Yeah, I feel a little sick."

"Well, okay." Jayla's face falls as she scrapes at her bowl, and I actually do start to feel sick.

Ellie's mom opens the driver's side of the Mini Cooper. I've only met her once, but I recognize her immediately. A tall, thin Latina woman with Ellie's wavy hair.

"Let's come back here another time," I say as I shove my arms into my jacket sleeves.

The passenger door of the blue car swings open.

I take a few steps backward and ram my thigh into the corner of a table. "I'm . . . *ouch* . . . I'm really sorry to run out on you like this. You can have the rest of my ice cream if you want."

"I don't like chocolate."

She doesn't like *chocolate*?

There's no time to ask questions.

"I'm really sorry," I repeat. "I'll see you at school on Monday, okay?" I slip out the back of the diner just as Ellie and her yellow scarf pop out of the car.

I loiter by the smelly dumpster until I think the coast is clear. Then I peek around the corner to make sure Ellie and her mom aren't still hanging around outside. The blue reindeer car seems to laugh at me. *You got yourself into this mess,* it says. It's right. The way I left Jayla was totally rude. What if she never talks to me again?

I hop on my bike and pedal as fast as my feet will take me. The cold air stings my face and dries out my eyes.

I'm ninety-six percent sure I escaped unseen. And since Ellie and Jayla never talk, Ellie will most likely never find out I was there.

I should feel relieved. Instead I feel worse than ever.

And the question remains: What do Duke and Paris have in store for me?

15
The Spelling-Bee Queen

In English on Monday, I run through some of Duke's possible payback methods: Trip me. Slash my suit. Pour hot gravy through my screen. I bet Paris will think up the idea, and Duke will deliver. They make the perfect evil duo.

The bell rings, and everyone crams out the door at once. It's like they think someone's passing out free tacos in the hall. I'm squeezing my way into the mob when Ms. Wu calls from behind.

"Ben, can I see you for a second?"

I fall back from the crowd and grip my binder. It's never a good sign when a teacher wants to talk to you in private.

Duke fist-bumps me on his way out. "Good luck, man."

I walk slowly up to Ms. Wu's desk, focusing on the

Gandalf bobblehead stationed next to her name plaque. "Am I in trouble or something?"

"No." She tilts her head, and her black bangs sway to the side. "The opposite, actually. Each teacher has been asked to encourage a couple of their students to run for next year's student council. I want to recommend you."

I look up. Me? Student council? Would people really vote for me?

"Your work is thorough," she says. "You work well in groups. I think you have great leadership potential."

I smile like a kindergartener who just got a gold star. I can't help it. A teacher hasn't ever taken me aside to compliment me before, especially not for "leadership potential."

"Thanks, Ms. Wu," I say. "I'm trying."

She lowers her voice like she has a secret. "I'm also impressed by how you've been befriending more people in the class. Some really need it."

I assume she's referring to Mitch. I've been trying to say hi to him every day before class starts. I even asked him to be my partner last Friday. Our assignment was to create a slideshow of pictures that represented our vocab words, but he showed me online pictures of quadcopter drones instead. I was pretty sure Ms. Wu saw him exit out of the drone tab as she paced down our aisle, but she never mentioned anything. Guess she didn't want to interrupt what she thought was our bonding time.

"It's no big deal." I flick Gandalf's head to watch it bobble. "I like your Gandalf, by the way."

She watches it bobble too, and her mouth curves into a smile. "You a *Lord of the Rings* fan?"

"I've read *The Hobbit* twice."

Her eyebrows shoot up. "Impressive."

"Not really." I shrug. "My friend Ellie has read the whole series."

"It's impressive nonetheless." She picks up a stack of papers on her desk and straightens them in front of her. "So, the student council information meeting is next Tuesday. You interested?"

"Sure. I guess it couldn't hurt to see what it's like." At my last school, I would have never considered running for student council. No one would have voted for me. Most people didn't know who I was. But things have changed. Duke's been talking to me. Jayla asked me to the dance. I'm starting to feel more comfortable in my classes. As long as no one finds out I'm the Spud, I might actually have a chance.

Ms. Wu jots down a reminder on a sticky note. "I'll get the form to you tomorrow. Now you better hurry to your next class or you'll be late."

I pull out my best Gandalf impression. "'A wizard is never late. Nor is he early. He arrives precisely when he means to.'"

She laughs. "See you tomorrow, Ben."

My worries about Duke float off my shoulders. For a moment I start to believe I'm a good person. Almost.

The feeling disappears when I step into the potato costume after school. The second I put on the head, still reeking of rotten ocean breeze, I'm reminded that I am, in fact, still a terrible person. Someone who lies to his family. Lies to his friends. Sure, I tried to redeem myself by being nice to Mitch, but Ms. Wu hasn't seen the behind-the-scenes action. The truth is, each time, before I say "hi" to him, my eyes automatically check to make sure Duke hasn't entered the classroom yet. And the one time I invited Mitch to be my partner was the day Duke just happened to be absent. I don't deserve to be in student council. I couldn't even lead the wave without falling on my face.

In the gym, I set my prop down and begin to practice, but all my wallowing makes it hard to get the moves right for my superstunt. It feels like lead is pulsing through my body and slowing it down. I take a deep breath and push out the negativity. I only have this afternoon and tomorrow to practice, and it has to be perfect. If I'm stuck being a potato, I might as well be the world's coolest potato. Not that I have much competition, as far as I'm aware.

My feet catch on, and my confidence starts climbing. Before I know it, I'm rocking the stunt. I'll probably become some sort of internet celebrity after people see this. I'll inspire bright-eyed new mascots the same way harness-swinging Wolf inspired me. Granted, I don't quite reach the same level of awesomeness as Wolf Man on Ice, but I'm doing the best I can. Maybe I'll even win over Duke and Paris. Maybe they'll be so impressed, they'll forget about the payback altogether. One can only hope.

• • •

Tuesday at lunch, Hunter tells me how before school, Lucy asked him to the dance by writing *DANCE?* on a Jenga block and dumping a pile of them in his locker. Apparently, all those two ever do together is play Jenga. Hunter's pretty stoked to answer her by spelling out "yes" in bacon.

I still haven't spoken with this Lucy girl, probably because she's partially homeschooled and only comes to school for choir, math, and history. Who knew middle school could be a part-time gig? I should look into that.

Hunter and I are debating whether or not bacon would leave grease stains on Lucy's patio (which it totally would, come on) when Ellie shows up, her eyes looking eager to reveal big news.

"Guys, guess what."

"Hmm . . ." Hunter rubs his chin. "Chicken butt?"

She gives him her *are you serious* face. "Chicken butt? Are we in second grade?"

"Ah, second grade." He stares wistfully into the distance. "That was a good year for me."

Ellie sweeps her braid over her shoulder as if literally brushing him off. "I think I might ask someone to the dance."

"Who?" I ask.

"Cole."

I focus on keeping a neutral expression. "Oh?"

"Yeah," she says. "I heard he'd been asked already, but yesterday in math he told me that the girl canceled on him because her family decided to go out of town."

Hunter sucks in through his teeth. "That stinks."

Ellie sits. "So, you guys think I should do it?"

Honestly, I don't. Something about the thought of

her dancing with Cole makes me wanna puke. But who am I to tell her what to do?

"Why not?" I say. "I mean, if you really want to. If there's literally no one else you'd rather go with."

She sighs big and heavy. "Seriously, what do you have against him?"

"Nothing! He's cool." I raise my palms and shrug. "There's just lots of cool people, and maybe you'd have a better time with someone else. I don't know."

She studies me like she's trying to read my mind, and I stare back with a poker face.

"Fun fact." Hunter pounds his water bottle between us. "I was the runner-up spelling-bee champion in second grade."

Ellie faces him. "You're still thinking about second grade over here?"

"Like I said, it was a good year for me. The girls chased me at recess and tried to kiss me."

I smirk. "Well, who wouldn't want to kiss a spelling-bee champion?"

"I was the champion in third grade," Ellie says, and then turns slightly pink. "Just saying."

I smother a smile with my fist. "What word did you win with?"

"'Crayon.'" She takes a sip of juice. "Everyone was spelling it without the *y*."

"That's such an easy word!" says Hunter.

Ellie pulls a sassy face. "Not as easy as the word *you* missed."

"It wasn't easy." He scowls.

"What was it?" I ask.

"'Chicken.'" His tone drips with resentment.

Ellie and I bust up laughing.

"Whatever," Hunter says. "Chick-*in*! It's a tough word! At least I knew there was a *c* in there somewhere."

Then Hunter goes on a rant about spelling bees, and how it's cruel and unusual punishment to place a kid in front of a crowd, force him to spell things autocorrect could do for him anyway, and watch him fail. I actually side with Hunter on this one. Ellie gets so heated in her defense of spelling bees that she accidentally flings her blueberry Go-Gurt onto my arm, which, on the bright side, is pretty tasty.

There's never a dull moment with my friends.

After school, I need to practice my superstunt before the big reveal tonight. But I also want to talk with Ellie. I decide to repeat what I did last Friday: I'll walk home with her and then run back to school to practice.

She might get suspicious if I'm always busy after school. Plus, I need to make sure she's coming tonight. She won't want to miss this.

I bring it up as we pass the stone house on our street corner. "So, are you going to the game?"

"Nah. No one can go." She kicks at some snow. "You're grounded, and Hunter's gonna be busy doing the bacon thing." At lunch Hunter begged her to help, but she felt it would be wrong to participate in bacon vandalism, so he's on his own. "Plus, I don't have a ride," she says. "Isn't it at Burrows?"

"No, didn't you hear the announcement? They switched it to home. The other school had scheduling conflicts."

"You pay attention to the school announcements?"

"Yeah." Ha. No. Coach told me earlier in the hall. "You know," I say, "if you go tonight, you can sit by Mitch. I told him to come."

"Really? Why?"

Yes, Ben. Why would you tell Mitch to come? Seriously, I need a collar to shock me every time I speak before thinking.

"Well," I say, inventing an excuse on the spot, "I think it's good for him to get out and do stuff. Be social." Who am I, his dad? In fact, I'm pretty sure my dad used that exact line on me back in California.

Ellie squints at me. "Do you want me to ask Mitch to the dance or something?"

I jerk my head toward her in surprise. "What? Why would I want you to ask Mitch?" I mean, he's better than Cole, but that still sounds like a terrible idea.

"I don't know. You're the one who wanted me to ask out Eric Daniels, the guy who dresses like he's going to church every day."

"I didn't say you should ask him out. I just thought you might like how . . . classy he is."

Her eyes become slits. "Why do you want me to sit with Mitch, then?"

I chew on my tongue. "I thought he could use a friend. Someone to sit by."

"Really?"

"Yeah." It's not really a lie—I do think he could use a friend. It's not the main reason I want her there, but still.

Ellie tugs at her yellow scarf. "That's really nice of you, Ben. Yeah, I guess I can go and look for him."

"Good," I say. "Plus, you'll get to see your *Cole*." My words come out more bitter than intended.

She lifts her chin. "I guess I will."

"So he's your type, then?" I blurt.

"Well, more so than Eric Daniels."

"But come on—*Cole*? How is he your type?"

Ellie huffs a small white cloud. "Why do you keep saying 'type,' like people can only like one type of person?"

"I don't know. People usually have a type. Don't they?"

"Okay, then. What's *your* type?"

I shrug. "Likes Slurpees?"

"For real."

I'm not sure I even know the answer to this question. "I guess someone I like being around. Someone I can talk to about whatever."

"You like being around Jayla?"

"Sure." The ice cream date was pretty fun. Until it exploded in my face, of course.

"And you can talk to her about whatever?"

"I don't know. I guess." The truth is, we haven't really talked much. And I always feel awkward when we do. But things might get better once I get to know her more. I haven't seen her since I ran out on her, but she accepted my apology over text.

Ellie looks smug, like she just won an argument, although I'm not sure what it was.

I pull up my hood. "So, how are you going to ask Cole?"

It's weird—as much as it annoys me to think about the guy, I keep bringing him up.

"Well," she says, "I was thinking about getting him a carton of buffalo wings. My mom said she'd take me to get some during lunch. Then I'd put them on his desk in math with a note that says, *I've never asked anyone to a dance before, so I'm just gonna 'wing' it.* Is that cheesy?"

I snicker. "Yeah, kinda." I mean, puns are always cheesy.

She stops walking. "Really?"

Now I feel bad for insulting her idea. "Well, it's cheesy, but that doesn't mean it's bad. I've heard of guys getting candy, but never wings." My mouth waters as I imagine spicy buffalo wings next to ranch sauce. "You know, the more I think about it, the cooler it is. I'm actually super jealous."

"Oh yeah?"

"Of the wings, yeah. You should get me some too."

She laughs. "That reminds me. I do have something for you." She digs in her side bag. "I was gonna give you this during lunch, but I didn't want Hunter to get jealous." She pulls out a sandwich bag and hands it to me.

It looks like she ripped up a plant and stuffed it in a bag. "You got me . . . leaves?"

"It's basil! I picked it off the plant for you to smell. Go ahead, take it out."

I bring one of the felty leaves to my nose and breathe in the soft, sweet scent. It's minty with a hint of pepper.

"So? Do you like it?" Her cheeks, rosy from the cold, dimple as she smiles.

I can't help but laugh. She's such a weirdo. "I love it. Thanks."

She lingers at her gate. "You know, it's really too bad you can't come to the game tonight."

"Yeah, I wish I could be there. You'll have to tell me how it goes."

She steps through the gate. "I'll tell you every detail."

Tonight the Spud has to win over Ellie, Duke, and the entire student body. Everything must go exactly as planned.

16
Shock and Awe

I lean my ear close to the metal gym door, listening to the pregame buzz on the other side. I hear chatter, trumpets, and the squeaks of sneakers against the court. My heart thumps along with the dribbling basketballs as players warm up. The announcer isn't calling me inside. Not yet. The stands are full, the band is playing; it'll be any minute now.

Earlier today, Coach Tudy instructed me to wait for the announcer's cue before going into the gym. He was as excited about my superstunt as I was, and insisted I perform it for the grand entrance. "Proud of you, boy," he said. "That's the kind of stuff we need around here." Our competitors, the Burrows Billy Goats, are favored to win. They've only lost one game the whole season. Our team has lost two, including the Jackrabbit disaster. We need all the momentum we can get.

"And now, everybody," the voice booms over the loudspeaker, "get up on your feet and give a warm welcome to our very own . . . Steeeeve the Spuuuuud!"

I kick open the doors and jog inside, blowing kisses like a Disney potato princess. The crowd eats it up. They cheer even louder as I hold my prop high above my head, the object I've loved for years but neglected for the past month: my skateboard.

I slip the red-rimmed board under my foot and propel myself across the gym.

I start with my signature move, which I mastered at age ten: the tiger claw. I stomp the board so it snaps into the air. I claw at it like a tiger reaching for its prey and flip it in a 360. With a flick of my wrist, I slip the board back under my feet and keep riding.

The cheers hit me at full volume. Duke's deep voice rings out above the rest: "Potato on wheeeeels! Yeah!"

His phrase catches on, and a chant starts up. *Potato on wheels. Potato on wheels. Potato on wheels.*

"I have more where that came from," I say, even though no one can possibly hear me.

I grapevine—right foot over left, left foot over right—all on top of the moving board. It's harder than you'd think since I have no view of my feet. At one point I step too far forward and almost lose my balance. I wobble on one leg, but by some freak force of nature I manage to stay upright. Victorious, I ride on, pumping my arms to the beat of the chant.

The loudest chanters by far are three kids near the back whose faces are painted red and black. Two of them are eighth graders I've seen around school, and the shortest one is the same little punk I was about to show up in the free-throw shoot-out two games ago. With war paint smeared over his chubby cheeks, he looks just like one of Peter Pan's Lost Boys.

I sail around the gym, swerving right, swerving left, and throwing in a bunny hop here and there. My legs move on their own without direction from my brain, like this is what they're meant to do. They've missed this freedom.

Time for the grand finale: a ghostride kickflip. I hop to the right of my board, run alongside it, and kick up the underbelly. The board does a side somersault in the air before I jump and slam it to the floor with both feet.

The bleachers explode with cheers. Even the players on the opposite team join in. Their mascot, a gray billy goat with a thin goatee, claps his hooves in approval. I raise my skateboard over my head and take a sweeping bow.

I search the audience. Ellie sits front and center in the section behind the band. Her smile lights up her whole face, and I can't help but feel proud I was the one who put it there. Beside her stands Mitch, who apparently recorded the whole thing, since he's holding his phone out in front of him. I'll have to ask him to send me the video later. Duke is up and hollering too. No way he'll want to get revenge on me now.

I sit on my bench, and the game starts on a positive note. Duke makes the first basket—a perfect layup—and we keep a steady lead throughout the first quarter. Cole attempts a few shots and misses horribly. We still keep the lead, just no thanks to Cole.

By the end of the second quarter, the Billy Goats have caught up. Our momentum could only last so long—after all, we're playing the great Burrows Middle School. Their star athlete, Ammon Hall, is making pretty much every three-pointer he attempts. Their mascot bleats loudly and leads their crowd in the wave. Unlike me, he doesn't trip and roll.

I do a double take at the scoreboard. I need to grab my potatoes before halftime. Coach told me earlier I only had to fill a few minutes, since the cheerleaders would be the main act, and I'm up first.

I sneak out to grab the potatoes I stored in the janitor's closet all week and return just in time. I carry the three large spuds to the center of the court and begin to juggle, keeping my moves basic. I can't track the potatoes with my eyes, so I rely a lot on muscle memory.

The cheers aren't as loud as they were for the skateboarding routine, but once I finish, almost everyone wears a *well, isn't that cute* smile. I don't know why, because if you think about it, it's actually quite messed up that I would toss my tater babies up in the air. That's child endangerment. I search for Ellie's smile again. Yep, there it is.

My potato babies and I return to our wobbly wooden bench as the cheerleaders line up in V formation. Jayla stands at the front of the V, hands on hips.

During the routine, I can't stop glancing back at Ellie and Mitch to spy on their interactions. Creepy, yes, but being in a mascot costume is probably the closest I'll ever get to being invisible while in plain sight, and I have to take advantage. Ellie and Mitch lean toward each other like they're in the middle of a serious conversation. What could they be talking about? Hopefully, nothing about me.

The whistle signals the start of the second half. The Spuds play at the top of their game, but it's barely enough to keep us competitive. The teams take turns nabbing the lead from each other, the outcome of the game impossible to predict.

At the end of the fourth quarter, the Billy Goats lead by one point, with ten seconds left on the clock. A quiet tension fills the air as everyone holds their breath. The ref's shrill whistle cuts through the silence.

Cole inbounds the ball to Seth Lopez, one of our most solid players. His eyes dart left and right, looking to pass to someone in a good position to score.

There's five seconds to go. I lean forward on my bench and press my fists to the Spud's mouth.

But the bench is too rickety. The wooden slab tilts forward under my weight. The potatoes beside me tumble several feet onto the court, right as Seth passes the ball to Duke. I cry out and scramble to grab them, but only manage to capture two.

Duke runs while dribbling the ball, about to make the winning shot. As if in slow motion, his left foot lands on baby spud number three. His legs buckle and he crashes to the floor, rolling onto his back like a dead beetle.

Duke's eyes scour the floor for the offending object until he finds the potato, which has skidded a few yards away as if running from the scene of the crime. Then he snaps his head toward me.

His face turns as red as his hair, and sweat drips from his forehead like he's literally melting from anger. His eyes burn with such a fury that I think I'm going to disintegrate, or at least turn into a french fry.

Coach paces the sidelines, pressing his hands to the sides of his head like he's juicing himself. Meanwhile, the crowd's booing is out of control. Their jeers hit me like bullets, and I resist the urge to duck and cover.

The ref calls interference and puts five seconds back on the clock, allowing us to repeat the play. Cole passes to Seth again, but this time around, the Goats make sure to guard him so he can't get in a good pass. He attempts the shot himself and misses, the final buzzer sounding with a score of 71–70, Billy Goats.

I don't turn to face the fans. I don't dare. My cheeks are about ten degrees from bursting into flames, and I feel heavy enough to sink through the floor—which would be great. I'd do anything to disappear.

Coach Tudy orders the team back to the locker room.

When Duke passes my bench, he checks to make sure Coach isn't looking and then shoves me so hard I nearly fall backward.

"Watch your back, Spudboy," he hisses as he walks away. So much for avoiding Duke's revenge plot.

Coach rounds up a couple of players who are arguing with the ref and ushers them out the door. I don't even want to think about what they're saying about me in the locker room.

I sit frozen on the bench as that achy, about-to-cry sensation creeps up my throat. I give up. No way in heck will I wear this costume ever again. Forget the fact that I shook on it with Coach in the principal's office. I'm done.

The crowds disperse, leaving just three straggling fans in the back row. I wish they'd hurry up and leave already so I can writhe my way out of this cursed suit and go curl up in my bed. Could things possibly get any worse?

Behind me, a high-pitched voice rings out from the stands.

"Get him!"

17
Attack of the Rabid Fans

The little Lost Boy look-alike rushes down the bleachers, his fierce eyes shining behind streaked war paint. His two older friends follow behind, leaping over the benches instead of taking the stairs. The taller of the two has arms so skinny I could probably roll over on them and they'd snap. The other boy, however, is basically a human pit bull. He growls through his teeth like I'm a juicy steak.

I snatch the skateboard from under the bench, my only hope for a quick escape. I press the board to my stomach, sprint a couple of steps, and belly flop onto the court. I sail toward the far doors like a penguin gliding down an iceberg as the boys chase me like leopard seals on the hunt.

I barrel-roll off my board just before it rams into the wall. Channeling all my ab strength, I wriggle onto my feet, only to feel a sharp kick in the meat of my calf.

The little monster sneers at me. "I've been in karate since I was six."

"Oh yeah?" I shoot back. "Well, I've been mashing potatoes since I was five!" I lurch at him as a threat. My foot yearns to deliver payback, but my brain stops me. I will not resort to kicking children. I will not.

A pair of sneakers squeaks behind me and I bolt. If either of the eighth graders catches me, who knows what they'll do? I zigzag around the gym, feeling like I'm playing a virtual-reality game where I can only see the screen in front of me as I'm chased from behind by killer zombies. Except the zombies are replaced by rabid sports fans, which are actually just as terrifying.

Pretty soon I can only manage a floppy jog. If I can just make it to the janitor's closet, I'll lock myself in until these guys are forced to leave out of starvation.

But I'm too slow. With only a few more strides till I reach the exit, the pit bull jumps on me and I crumple to the floor. "Hold his arms down!" he orders his friend while turning me onto my back.

The skinny boy pins my wrists, and the Lost Boy jabs my plushy stomach with his little fists. It feels like being kicked in the stomach by a baby marshmallow.

I lie limp as a noodle, too tired to fight back. It's over.

The pit bull tugs my head. "It. Won't. Come. Off," he grunts.

"There's a metal thing!" the skinny boy says.

"Huh?"

"You know, the clicky metal thing."

"What are you talking about?"

"That thing on the side of the head! Look!"

Click! One of the boys—I can't see which—unsnaps the suit's side latches. They're gonna tell everyone about this at school. I close my eyes and brace for the big reveal.

"JARED AND DALLIN! OVER HERE. NOW." A voice explodes from the doorway, echoing its way around the gym. Coach Tudy has returned, and just in time.

The older boys freeze, and the little one lets out a sharp gasp.

"I said, NOW."

The boys shuffle toward the coach.

My ears burn like hot coals as I stare at the ceiling. This is not a position I'm proud to have found myself in. Literally and figuratively.

"Do you know what kind of racket you boys are causing?" Coach roars. "We can hear it from the locker room!"

I can't see the boys' faces, but I can imagine how they must look—all lined up, shoulders hunched, and eyes staring at the floor like puppies caught peeing on the carpet.

"Sorry, Uncle Gordon," the pit bull and the Lost Boy mutter in unison.

Uncle Gordon? I guess those two do look somewhat like miniature versions of Coach. If I weren't so miserable, I'd probably crack up. But even my lip muscles are too tired to move.

Coach speaks through clenched teeth. "Your father will be hearing about this, boys. Get out. And your friend too."

Three pairs of feet scuttle out the door, leaving just Coach Tudy and me in tense silence. This would be the perfect opportunity for him to murder me since he just banished the only available witnesses.

My throat swells and sweat stings my eyes. "Thanks," I manage.

He lets out a deep rumbling grunt. "One more game, Hardy. Student council will be in charge of halftime, so we'll just need you on the sidelines." He tromps over to the exit. "And *don't* bring back the potatoes." The door echoes as it slams behind him.

Left alone in the gym, I close my eyes and take a few deep breaths to slow down my pounding chest. *In . . . out . . . in . . . out.*

I heave myself to my feet and try my best not to collapse back onto the floor. I can't believe Coach tried pulling the whole "one more game" thing. Yeah, right! If I weren't sure before, I am now: No way am I coming back. I'll take my suspension. I'll miss the dance.

But that decision doesn't feel right either. Nothing does.

Coach Tudy could have let those guys pull off my mask and ruin my life. It would've been perfect payback for me screwing up the game, and possibly his chance at retirement. Instead he rescued me. If I bailed on him now, it'd be spitting in his face. *Never give up,* he said. *No matter how bad things get.* Surely he didn't know things would get *this* bad.

I square my shoulders and tell myself it'll be okay. Sometimes the easiest person to lie to is yourself.

I pick up my board and head out the door. One more

game. I can survive one more game. I just have to stay near Coach for protection and avoid getting fancy with my tricks. What happened tonight will smooth itself out soon enough. I mean, it's middle school; we all have short attention spans.

Everyone will forget about this by tomorrow. Right?

18

South Fork's Most Wanted

As I exit my first period the next morning, a flyer in the hall stops me in my tracks. A cartoon Mr. Potato Head stares me in the face. Above his head the word WANTED screams in a large, bold font.

Down the hall, several of the flyers hang slightly askew, each stuck to the wall with a piece of masking tape. These weren't up before school, were they? I rip one off and read it:

"Pretty dumb, huh?"

I whirl around. Jayla flinches and lets out a short burst of laughter. "Wow, *someone's* jumpy today."

I fake a laugh, but not very well.

She brushes my arm with her fingertips. "Calm down. I'm not that scary."

My arm tingles with goose bumps. I open my mouth, but nothing comes out.

Jayla nods at the flyer in my hand. "So, what do you think?"

"What? Oh, this? Yeah, I just. I thought it was. Like, why a potato? And so I grabbed it."

She smirks. "Yeah, Duke made that, so of course he had to use the word 'poop.'" She rolls her eyes, and her eyelids shimmer with gold. "It's just, like, weird, you know. I swear I know everyone at this school, but I've never heard of a Doug."

I hesitate before my next question, afraid of the answer. I lift the flyer. "Are you helping with this?"

She glances down, and I almost sense some embarrassment. "Duke and Paris are more into it than I am. They snuck out of first period together to hang up the flyers." She looks back up and any hint of shame is gone. "I hope they catch him, though."

"Yeah, me too." Ugh.

She shifts her binder to her other arm. "So, did you hear that Seth got asked to the dance?"

I try to look interested. "No way!"

Jayla keeps telling me about who's going to the dance with who. I try to pay attention, but her words all blur together, and the only thing I can think about is the flyer in my hand. I read over it again, the question bubbling up inside: What in the world are these people going to *do* to me? But I missed my opportunity to ask. The conversation has veered so far away from the mascot subject that it'd be weird if I went back to it. If I look too interested in the fate of "Doug," Jayla might get suspicious.

The bell rings right before I reach my Spanish classroom. I groan out loud. This is just what I need today. A tardy. Hopefully, it's one of Ms. Hart's good days. Sometimes she gets super upset when people are late, and other times it's like she forgets she cares. I walk through the door feeling like I'm on some game show: *And what's behiiiiiind door number two?*

Luckily, a few girls are chatting with Ms. Hart by her desk, so I'm able to slip in unnoticed. Even better, almost everyone's out of their seats. I nod to Ellie on the far side of the room and head her way, knowing I can't get in trouble if class hasn't really started yet. The desk in front of her is empty, so I sit in it and turn around.

"Whatcha reading?" I ask.

She looks up. "*Goblet of Fire.*" She holds up the cover. "Aka the best Harry Potter book."

I smack my hand over my heart and pretend to look offended. "I mean, it's good, but definitely not as good as *Prisoner of Azkaban.*"

"Not even!" She scoffs playfully. "Does Harry fight a dragon in that one? I think not."

"But he saves a hippogriff. And hippogriffs are cooler than dragons."

She slams her book down. "All right, now it's personal."

I laugh. We probably sound super nerdy to the people sitting behind us. I glance back to see if they're listening and catch a bit of their conversation.

"Did you see Duke's face after he fell?" says this girl named Tanna who glues boy-band pictures to all her binders. "He looked like he was going to start shooting lava out of his head."

"I don't blame him!" says the kid sitting next to her. "It was all the Spud's fault."

"Yeah," says a grumpy-faced dude from the row over. "We had that game in the bag!"

The voices talk over each other, all swirling together and making my brain ache:

"He started out cool with the skateboard thing, and then he just failed."

"It was pretty pathetic, right?"

"Think they'll find him?"

"I've never heard of a Doug."

Ellie turns around in her seat to join the mascot conversation.

"Why is everyone hating so much on the Spud?" she says. My eyebrows jerk in surprise. It's a total Ellie thing to say—but not in front of people she's not close with.

"I saw what happened," she says. "It was an accident."

"An accident that cost us the game," the grumpy dude says.

"Come on," Ellie says. "You don't know Duke would've made that shot anyway."

"Of course he woulda! Back me up, Ben."

My jaw drops a little, releasing this stupid "uhhhhh" sound. Then I remember I don't have to pick a side; I have the perfect cop-out: "I wasn't there. I can't say."

"Well, I just think everyone needs to let it go." Ellie grips the top of her chair. "Whoever put those flyers up is an idiot."

"It was Duke," I say.

"Case in point." Her eyes widen, and I can tell that she didn't mean to say that last bit out loud. I smother a laugh. She's probably all racked with guilt now.

"Okay, everyone, to your seats. *¡Siéntense!*" Ms. Hart swings her hands at us like she's conducting a choir.

Throughout the period, my eyes keep glancing at Ellie as she twirls her pencil at her desk. Why didn't I agree with her during the conversation? Why was she quicker to defend me than I was to defend myself? And why am I so convinced it'd look fishy for me to speak out for Doug? Is it really that out of character for me to defend someone?

I mentally replay what might have happened earlier if I weren't such a wimp:

GRUMPY DUDE: Back me up, Ben.

BEN: I can't. Ellie's right. I didn't see what happened, but everyone should show a little more mercy.

ELLIE: *(smiling at Ben)* I knew there was a reason I liked you.

I clench my eyes shut. I blew it. I glance at Ellie again. She's finished her worksheet early and is back to the book, her eyes widening and narrowing as she reads.

Suddenly my stomach churns. Today's the day. The day she's going to ask Cole to the dance.

• • •

Something funky's going on with my taste buds. I usually love graham crackers, but today at lunch they taste like the wood shavings at the bottom of a hamster cage. Ellie's mom checked her out of lunch to get wings for Cole, so at the table it's just me, Hunter, and Lucy—his curly-haired, Jenga-playing, almost girlfriend. Usually, Lucy goes home after third period, but I guess she was so impressed with Hunter's bacon answer last night that she couldn't get enough of him. (Side note: Hunter's mom forced him to lay the bacon out on tinfoil, so no staining of concrete ever occurred. Huzzah.)

Since neither Hunter nor Lucy went to the basketball game, the mascot subject doesn't come up at all. Instead they get into a pretty heated debate over whether Monopoly is better than Settlers of Catan. I mean, I like board games as much as the next guy (assuming the next guy likes board games a medium amount), but it's not the most exciting subject, nor one I have much to say about, so I kind of feel like a third wheel.

I get to English early, go straight to my back corner, and stare at the scratches on the surface of my desk. Some bored kid from another period has etched a bunch of little checkerboards into the hard plastic. I run my fingers over the grooves, thinking about this thing I read on the internet once. It said that if you fake a smile, your brain makes chemicals to trick yourself into feeling happy—kind of like how exercise releases endorphins that improve your mood. I tighten the corners of my mouth and force them upward for a couple of seconds, but they drop back down like they have tiny weights attached to them. Life tip: Never believe what you read on the internet.

"Benny boy!" Duke grins down at me.

I strain another fake smile, the corners of my mouth still struggling.

He slaps my desk. "I hear you and Jayla are a thing."

I lift my chin. "Yeah, man."

"That's sweet, dude. Congrats." He holds out his hand, and I slap it.

From the corner of my eye, I notice Mitch stiffen. His head turns slightly in our direction as if he's trying to eavesdrop.

Duke grabs my shoulder. "You gotta eat lunch with us, man. Jayla and Paris started sitting at our table."

"Yeah. Yeah, maybe." The funny thing is, if he knew I was Doug the Spud, he wouldn't be asking me to sit with them. Not a chance.

"Duke, to your seat." Ms. Wu points at Duke, then shakes her head at a kid in the front row. "Joshua, salami away." She mutters under her breath, "Why is that even a thing?"

During class, a billion thoughts race through my head—the wanted posters, Jayla touching my arm, Ellie standing up for the Spud, becoming Hunter's third wheel, chicken wings, Mr. Potato Head, and Friday's game. What kind of humiliation do Duke and company have planned for me? I have to constantly be on guard. What if they try to pin me down and pull off my head, like the rabid fans at last night's game? If so, I can put up a fight. I've had practice. And as long as Coach is in the gym, he'd rescue me again. Wouldn't he?

After class, I turn in a blank worksheet to the classwork bin and wait for the crowds in the doorway to subside. Mitch pops up beside me, looking extra small in his puffy orange jacket. "Hey, sorry about the posters, man. I swear I haven't told anyone about . . . you know, how you're . . . you know."

"Mm-hmm," I hum. I don't feel like talking about it.

"Are you okay? You look super depressed."

Way to rub it in, Mitch. Is he trying to make me feel worse?

He trails me into the hall. "You know, I wasn't gonna tell you this, but . . . but . . ."

I stop walking. "What?"

"Uh. Forget it."

"Come on. You can't start a sentence like that and just stop." I lean my shoulder against a locker. "What?"

"I sat by Ellie at the game last night."

My brain stops my mouth just as I'm about to say *I know* and replaces the words with "Oh yeah?" Turns out, deception is a learned skill, just like anything else.

"Yeah," continues Mitch. "We were talking about you."

I remember seeing them talking in the bleachers. He better not have said anything embarrassing. "What'd you say?"

"I asked her if she liked you."

"*What?*" For a second, my heart stops. "Why'd you ask that? That's, like, so second-grade."

"Then I guess you don't care what she said," he says with a smug grin.

"You're right. I don't," I bluff. He'll spill eventually.

We walk in silence, but the suspense is killing me. I do

care, and Mitch knows it. He's dangling the information in front of me like a doughnut on a string.

I give in. "Fine, you win. What did she say?"

Mitch lifts his eyebrows, wrinkles forming on his forehead. "She said *maybe.*"

"Maybe?" My stomach does this weird fluttery thing. Kind of like there are butterflies in there, or maybe angry moths.

"Yeah. Maybe."

I look straight ahead so he can't read my expression. "That doesn't mean anything."

"Well, she could have said no."

"Mitch, why are you telling me this?"

"I don't know. You looked sad, so I thought it might cheer you up."

I nudge him with my elbow and shake my head. "Dude, you're weird."

We part ways at the corner, and as I walk to my next class, something strange happens. Something I didn't expect.

I smile for the first time all day.

19
Dads Can Be Cool Sometimes

After school, I wait by the bike racks, but there's no sign of Ellie. She's usually here by now. I reach for my phone and half complete a "where are you?" text before I remember her phone is still nonfunctional from its milk bath. And besides, she's tutoring. One more week and I can tutor too. Then I won't have to walk alone anymore.

When I get home, I go to my room and dig out my math notes. I can't believe I'm saying this, but I really need to study. Not only do I have a test coming up on Friday, but if I'm going to start tutoring, I need to get better at geometry in case someone brings math homework in.

I've just cleared some T-shirts off my desk when Dad knocks on my door. "Hey, buddy, can I talk to you for a minute?" His voice sounds a little strained, like he's got something caught in his throat.

My heart speeds up to a wary jog. Usually it's Mom who checks on me after school. I try to think if I did anything that might have gotten me in trouble. Did I break something? Forget to feed Buster? "Yeah, come in."

Dad enters and flashes me a fake-looking smile, like the ones you see on dentist office ads. "You studying?"

I nod at my notes. "Yeah."

"That's good." He sits on my beanbag and runs a hand through his hair. "What are you learning about?"

We talk about my math class for a bit. Dad's especially interested in math since he's an electrical engineer. Too bad I don't seem to have inherited his mathematical brains. Then we talk about my other classes—how we're reading *Ghost* in English, and how Ms. Funk showed us her dead-beetle collection in science. This shouldn't feel weird, but for some reason it does. Like, it'd be totally normal for Dad to ask me about school over dinner or something, but he doesn't usually come into my room just to chat.

I cut to the chase. "So, what did you want to talk about?"

Dad tugs at his collar. "Just . . . this. I wanted to check in. See how things are."

Riiight.

He draws in his eyebrows. "Look, Ben."

Here it comes.

"I just got an email from your English teacher. She said you turned in a blank worksheet today, which is unusual behavior for you. She's worried about you." He squints a little. "I'm wondering if I should be too."

"Oh." I look away and start messing around with my fidget spinner. "I was just really tired today. I didn't feel like doing a worksheet." He doesn't need to know all the details. He only came up here because my teacher emailed him. He was guilted into it.

Dad stays quiet for a while, and all I can hear is the hum of the heater. Finally he takes a deep breath.

"Ben, I want to apologize. I know I haven't been as present lately. I've been stressed about the move, stressed about fixing up the house. And this new job is kicking my butt." He lowers his voice and winks. "Don't tell Mom I said 'butt.'"

I can't help but smile. Even though I'm twelve, Mom still treats the words "butt" and "fart" like swear words. I haven't heard Dad crack a joke in a while. I realize how much I've missed that.

Dad leans forward and rests his chin on his fists. "Has the move been hard on you, too?"

"It has," I admit. I put down the fidget spinner and meet his eyes. "Honestly, it wasn't too bad at first. I mean, it's insanely cold, but other than that, it was all right. But lately, it's gotten harder." At my last school, I didn't like being the kid who flew under the radar, but that was a whole lot better than having a literal reward out for my capture.

Dad rubs his stubbly chin. "Why has it gotten harder?"

"I don't know." I shrug. "I guess everything's just sinking in. This is where we live now. I'll never get my old room back. Or get to visit the beach on weekends." That's not the whole truth, but I don't know if I'm ready to spill about the mascot drama. It's so embarrassing.

I twist my fidget spinner again. It was pretty cool of Dad to come talk to me, though. Maybe I should tell him. . . .

There's raspy breathing on the other side of the door. "Abby!" I yell. I leap out of my chair and swing open the door. Abby smiles sheepishly up at me.

"You were eavesdropping!" I was about to tell Dad about being the Spud. She could have heard everything!

"Calm down, Ben." Dad stands and narrows his eyes at Abby. "Is that true?"

She shakes her head vigorously. "I was just coming up here to tell you to take me to my violin lesson."

I scoff. "Yeah, sure."

"It's true!" She flings her arms around. "Mom's still working on the website. She needs Dad to take me!"

Mom's a website designer, and she's been working on a project all day. Abby's got a good excuse, but I don't buy it. She might have come up here to get Dad, but she decided to lurk at the door when she heard us talking.

"You're always trying to snoop around my business!" I say.

Dad rests a firm hand on my shoulder. "Ben, get back to studying. Abby, let's go."

Dad leaves to take Abby to her violin lesson, and I stay in my room. After fuming for a minute about Abby and her nosiness, I start to study. For the first time since I moved here, I actually study. It's nothing short of a miracle. There's one tricky bit, though, that I'm not quite getting.

Ellie would know the answer. Maybe I can get to school early tomorrow and ask her for help. At least that's one thing I can look forward to.

• • •

My phone alarm buzzes at six-forty-five the next morning, fifteen minutes earlier than usual. I pop out of bed like a piece of toast. I can't be late to school.

After a quick shower, I put gel in my hair, which I never do. I don't know why, but it's a feel-good kind of day. The type of day where you want to look nice, just because.

I dig around the medicine cabinet for the aftershave my cousin Angelo got me at the family gift exchange last Christmas. The tiny glass container is hidden behind my sister's glitter nail polish. I dab a little onto my cheeks, and my skin tingles as it soaks up the earthy musk. I smell like a rugged mountain man. Why don't I wear this stuff more often? I pour more onto my fingers and massage it over my jawline.

On my way to school, the scent starts to make me feel dizzy. I scoop up some snow to wash the smell off my hands. Then I dry my hands on my jeans, which only makes the odor seep into my clothes. I might as well have a hundred car fresheners around my neck. It's official: I'll never wear aftershave again.

On campus, I gauge the expression of the people I pass to see if they react to my smell. A guy with bulky headphones walks by. No expression change whatsoever.

A girl in a purple coat walks my way next. As we cross paths, I swerve close to her and observe her face. She shoots me an awkward half smile. Oh no—she probably thought I was flirting! This plan is not working.

When I walk into the building, I see Ellie, Hunter, and Lucy grouping together in front of the media center bench. Ellie bounces on the balls of her feet, hands in the pockets of her blue coat.

I walk up to the group and stop a few feet away so I don't overpower them with my smell. "Hey, guys. What's up?"

Three silent heads swivel toward me.

Ellie and Lucy exchange that same telepathic-girl glance that Paris and Jayla sometimes share. What mental messages are they communicating? That I smell like a walking cologne sample? I take a step back.

"Why are you standing so far away?" asks Hunter.

"Oh, I don't know." I shuffle forward a couple of feet.

Lucy rests her hand on Hunter's arm. "So, Hunt. I'm gonna get a bagel. I forgot to eat breakfast."

"*Hunt,* huh?" I say. "Can I start calling you that too?" I chuckle but stop short when no one laughs along. Lucy's is the only expression that resembles a smile, but her

half smirk seems more to say, *Dude, I'm really glad I'm not you right now.*

Hunter snatches up his backpack. "I'll buy it for you," he says to Lucy, and the two walk off, leaving me and Ellie alone.

Ellie suddenly becomes very interested in her fingernails.

"I like your nails," I say, noticing they're red.

"Yeah. The color is chipped." There's something flat in her tone, something devoid of its usual warmth.

I tug at my collar. My nonconfrontational side is setting off warning signals in my head: *Awkward alert! Evacuate the premises!* But my curiosity keeps my feet grounded in place. "Is something wrong?"

Ellie folds her arms. "Ben, we know you're not grounded."

The temperature around me plummets a thousand degrees. This can't be happening. How much does she know? I focus on the library poster, the lump in my throat making it nearly impossible to speak. "Who told you? Mitch?"

"Mitch? What? No, I saw your mom at lunch yesterday."

"My mom?"

"Yeah, when I was getting wings."

"My mom was getting wings?"

"I don't know what she got. We were at the same restaurant."

"My mom was at a restaurant?"

She rolls her eyes so hard her head leans back. "Is this what you do when you're caught in a lie? Just turn everything I say into a question?"

"Was I asking questions?"

Ellie puts one hand on her hip. "Your mom asked me why I hadn't been around lately. She said I should stop by."

I swallow. I can see where this is going.

"So," she continues, "I asked, 'Isn't Ben grounded?' And she was all, 'No. Should he be?' I made up some excuse about how I must've been thinking of someone else. I still don't know why I covered for you."

I check that no one's watching us. "Ellie, it's not what you think."

"Are you grounded or not?"

"Well, no—"

"Then it's exactly what I think." She sighs. "I mean, if you don't wanna hang out with us, you don't have to lie."

"But that's not—" I try to explain, but she keeps talking.

"What have you been doing these past two weeks? I

mean, I overheard you took Jayla out for ice cream last weekend, but I figured you just snuck out like you did for my recital. Turns out you were never even grounded at all. I guess that's just what you'd rather be doing—hanging out with 'cool' people like her."

"It's not like that." The bell rings, but I wouldn't have been able to say more anyway.

"I have to go," Ellie says, her voice catching slightly. She sweeps her book bag up from the bench and slings it over her shoulder. She hustles away, her long hair swinging behind her.

I stay frozen and watch her leave, feeling like stale old gum that's stuck to the bottom of a shoe. Things couldn't have gone more perfectly wrong.

My double life as a potato has ruined a lot of things for me. It's ruined my love of juggling. It's ruined my love of skateboarding. It's ruined my love of chicken wings. But I never expected it to ruin my friendships. All I wanted was for these games to go by quickly and quietly—not for them to destroy my life.

Things have gone too far. I'm not sure how I'm going to fix this, but one thing's for sure. It's time to come clean.

20
The Realization

At lunch, I walk into the cafeteria without a solid plan. I'm ready to reveal my secret identity to my friends, but I haven't decided if the cafeteria is the right place to do it. In such a crowded area, anyone could overhear.

I crane my neck for a glimpse of my lunch table but can't see through the crowds. I weave my way across the room, hoping Hunter and Ellie haven't found a new place to eat in order to avoid me.

I catch sight of our table. Hunter and Ellie are there, but so is Lucy, who giggles and reaches across the table to ruffle Hunter's hair. Ugh. Is she really going to be sitting with us from now on?

I imagine our trio becoming a foursome, and it just feels wrong. Three is like the standard number for tight-knit best friends. It's practically a universal rule—look at the Three Musketeers, the Three Stooges, the Three Blind Mice (but I'm not sure I want to end up like them).

The three new best buds laugh together over some apparently hilarious story Hunter is telling, and it hits me: There's no room for a fourth member of the group. And the member who got kicked out is me.

That does it. I can't reveal my secret identity right now. Not with Lucy around. Something tells me she can't be trusted. Maybe it was the way she looked at me when she claimed she "wanted a bagel." She probably doesn't even like bagels.

Mid-laugh, Ellie catches me staring at them. We lock eyes for half a second before she snaps her head away. Where do I go from here? I can either join them and be treated like I have the plague or walk away and look like a wimp who can't bear confrontation. Lose, lose.

I need to stall.

Enter: the vending machine.

I dig through my pockets for extra change and come up empty-handed. I'll have to mime inserting a quarter, and then pretend my chips got stuck. I eye the assortment of chips and vitamin waters, deciding which item to fake select.

A deep voice calls from the middle of the cafeteria. "Benny boy!"

Duke waves to me from his table, a couple of rows down from my usual spot. "Come sit with us!"

The table looks crowded as is. There are about ten guys, all members of the basketball team, and squished in the middle are the two new additions: Jayla and Paris.

Paris scoots over on the bench, leaving an empty space for me next to Jayla. She points to the spot and mouths the words, *Sit here.*

I've always wondered what it would feel like to eat at the basketball table. Sitting squished next to Jayla doesn't sound so bad, either. I walk over and slide into the spot next to her and manage a smile. My friends may have rejected me, but at least I have other options.

Ellie turns her head to the side, holding her chin out straight and stiff. She hates me. I know it.

"Don't you have anything to eat?" Jayla asks. She smells like peach and vanilla, which reminds me: I'm starving.

I look at my hands as if expecting food to suddenly appear in them. "My food got stuck in the vending machine."

Paris rests on her elbows. "We can get someone to knock it out for you."

"No, thanks," I say. "I'm not hungry."

"A guy as big as you?" asks Jayla. "How are you not hungry?"

I straighten my spine. She thinks I'm big? Compared to her, I guess I am. Maybe the dumbbells I sometimes lift before bed are more effective than I thought.

While I'm here, I might as well do some digging to see what Duke has planned for the mascot. But how can I bring it up casually? Naturally?

Paris is eating potato chips. Jackpot.

"Hey, Paris," I say. "Can I have some of your chips?"

She holds out her bag. "Thought you weren't hungry."

"I can't resist potato chips," I lie, biting into the nasty salt-and-vinegar flavor. "Speaking of potatoes . . ."

Paris smirks. "Speaking of potatoes?"

"Yeah. It just reminded me. You're looking for the Spud mascot, right?"

"Yeah." She leans in closer. "You know him?"

"No. Not at all. I was just wondering what was gonna happen once you find him."

Her eyebrow arches like a villain's in a comic book. "Let's just say you'll want to be at the game on Friday. It's gonna be good."

The game on Friday. The last game of the season. Of course the payback will happen there. It's the perfect place to humiliate the mascot. The whole school will be watching.

My stomach suddenly feels very heavy, despite only having eaten chips. "But what are you going to do, exactly?" I ask.

"You'll see," she says in a tone that tells me I better not ask again. It's obvious I'm not getting any more out of her than that.

Duke yells down the table to no one in particular. "Guys, look! A meat burrito!" He wraps a slice of pizza around a stick of salami and waves it in the air. "But wait," he says. "Needs some salsa." He empties a packet of mustard over his "burrito," and the guys around him hee-haw like donkeys.

Cole's cackly laughter rings out above the rest. He sits on the other side of Jayla. Ellie never told me for sure if she followed through with asking him to the dance.

I lean back to call down the table. "Hey, Cole."

He reluctantly shifts his attention from Duke to me.

"You're going to the dance with Ellie, right?"

Jayla and Paris gape at each other.

"Oh yeah." Cole scratches his neck and steals a side glance at the girls. "It, like, just happened yesterday, so I haven't really told anyone yet. But Ellie's chill. You guys are tight, right?"

"Pretty tight." At least we used to be. My stomach clenches and my ears burn. Cole will probably replace me as Ellie's best friend. *Cole,* who doesn't deserve her friendship. He hasn't even told anyone she asked him to the dance, like he doesn't even care.

"This is how you get your protein in!" Duke is a few bites into his burrito creation.

Seth Lopez shoves a hot dog up to Duke's face like it's a paper he wants autographed. "Duke, take this! Stick this in the pizza too!"

Duke wrinkles his nose. "This?" He snags the dog and flings it over his shoulder. "I'm not adding that—that's gross."

Look at that: Even Duke has food standards.

The hot dog bounces a couple of tables away and rolls up beside Hunter's foot. He stares at it but doesn't pick it up. Our hot-dog-chucking days are long gone. I don't know if we'll ever get them back.

I look over to Ellie and catch her eye. This time she doesn't jerk her head away, and neither do I. Instead we hold each other's gaze for about three whole seconds. In that time, she somehow reassures me that she doesn't actually hate me. She looks sad, not angry.

I want to go sit with her. I wonder if she can tell.

As I listen to the chatter at my new table, I realize

something. I'm exactly where I always thought I wanted to be. Jayla is on my left, and the basketball crowd is on my right. And yet here I am, when I should be happy, wanting to leave. Wanting to be at my old table.

A new realization hits. No—it more than hits. It smacks me across the face. It zaps me like an electric fly swatter. It bulldozes me over, kicks me in the shin, and screams in my ear: I like Ellie. I *more* than like her. It's the kind of like that hums in my ears and turns my chest into a giant balloon that's one puff away from bursting.

I don't just like Ellie. I *like* like her. Oh no.

How did I not notice this before? It's so obvious. When I'm with Ellie, I feel happy. I feel like myself. I feel not-like-right-now. If I'd been smart enough to realize this earlier, maybe I'd be going to the dance with her instead of with Jayla.

What would she say if I told her? Would she ever choose me over Cole?

It's a slim chance, but if I never try, I'll never know. It's not enough to tell her I'm the Spud. I have to tell her how I feel.

21
~~Love~~ Letters

That night, I sit on my bed scrawling out the most pathetic letter of my life.

I read over what I have written so far:

Dear Ellie,

Wait, "dear"? What is she, my pen pal? I scratch out the word and start again.

~~Dear~~ Ellie,

This may come as a shock to you, but the truth is, I have been Steve the Spud for the past two weeks. Super embarrassing, I know. Especially now that the whole school hates me.

That's why I pretended to be grounded. I really

should have told you from the start. But I am a terrible person, and so I didn't. I'm sorry.

I also wanted to talk to you about Jayla. At first, I was excited about the dance. But the thing is, I don't feel the same way anymore . . .

That's all I've got. I cringe at the thought of Ellie reading this. But I forge onward, tacking on a sentence that I know immediately I'll have to rewrite:

I have started to realize that I like you more

Ughhh. "I like you more"? I sound like a six-year-old. How can I word this better?

I have started to realize that I ~~like you more~~ think about you a lot

Too creepy.

I have started to realize that I ~~like you more think about you a lot~~ miss your company

Too formal.

I have started to ~~realize that I like you more think about you a lot miss your company~~ wonder if we could ever be more than friends

Sounds like a cheesy One Direction song.

I have started to ~~realize that I like you more think about you a lot miss your company wonder if we could ever be more than friends~~ notice how pretty you are

No. Just, no.
Maybe I could be poetic about it. Use a metaphor.

~~I have started to realize that I like you more think about you a lot miss your company wonder if we could ever be more than friends notice how pretty you are~~
You know how in a potato field, you can't see the potatoes growing because they're hiding underground? Well, that could represent how sometimes things develop without you even noticing. Then one day, you dig it up, and boom, it's there. Like my feelings for you . . .

BAD. BAD. BAD.

I crumple the sheet and chuck it into the mini trash can by my desk. No more letter writing for me. I'll give Ellie the message in person. And just the first part about me being the potato, *not* the mushy stuff. I don't know what I was thinking. Telling her I like her would only make things awkward between us and completely ruin our friendship.

I hop off my bed and dig the note back out of the trash can, worried that my sister will somehow get hold of it. I wouldn't put it past her to dig through my trash. This letter would give her blackmail on me for the rest of my life.

It must be destroyed.

"Ben!" Mom's voice floats up the stairs. "Time for dinner!"

"One second!" I hurdle over my bed with the note in hand and scour the top of my dresser for the little red lighter that Dad bought me once for a camping trip. I shuffle some books around but can't find it. I could have sworn I'd left it here.

I search for a spot of red like I'm playing I Spy. *I Spy with my little eye something that is . . .*

Green! Turns out it's a green lighter. It's camouflaging itself on top of the green beanie on my nightstand.

"Ben!" Mom persists.

“Coming!” I snatch the lighter and hold it to the corner of my letter. I flick on the flame and let it lick up all evidence of my pathetic confession. A soft smell of smoke fills the room as my words transform into bits of ash drifting to the floor.

“Ben.” Mom swings the door open and pokes her head inside. I startle and drop the half-devoured sheet of paper. I catch it midair with my other hand and shake it violently until the flames go out.

“What in the world are you doing?” She peers over my bed at the ash-covered carpet.

“Just. Um. Playing with fire.” I drop the last scrap to the floor and cringe.

Her tone hardens. “Are those *ashes* on the floor?”

“I was just going to vacuum them up.”

She crosses her arms. “We do not light *fires* in this house. Understand?”

I nod vigorously.

She blows a wavy strand of hair out of her face. “You can vacuum after dinner. We’re all waiting on you.”

All the way down the stairs, she rattles on about how I need to have better respect for property and my room is a disaster and fire is not a toy and yada yada. At least she didn’t ground me. Not that it would make a difference, since I have no one to hang out with anyway.

We join Dad and Abby at the perfectly set table. Dad prays and we dig in—roast beef, steamed carrots, and Mom's signature gluey mashed potatoes. I fork up a few slices of roast beef.

Mom glances at my plate. "Take some potatoes and carrots, Ben."

I swallow. "No thanks. I'm on this new diet where I have to be purely carnivorous."

Dad puts on a stern expression. "Listen to your mother, Ben." He's probably thinking, *If I have to eat this, so do you.*

Mom slops a huge serving of potatoes onto my plate, giving me extra, most likely as punishment for playing with fire.

"Look how Abby is eating so many carrots!" Mom says. She seems to have forgotten that Abby is ten, not four. But her praise-the-good-behavior trick works nonetheless, and Abby dishes up even more carrots.

"I did really well on my chair test today!" pipes Abby. "I made it to first stand with Brielle Mendoza! She's really nice. She's helping me with my scales."

"That's great," I say, muscling a smile. Mom and Dad light up. I'm really happy for Abby. Her hard work is paying off. At least one of us is settling in here.

Then I zone out while Mom and Dad talk about boring stuff like Mom's website designing and how Dad's supervisor is a jerk. If Dad hates his job so much, I don't get why we can't just move back to California. The only thing I liked about Idaho was Hunter and Ellie, and now they hate my guts.

"Want to shoot some hoops after dinner?" Dad asks. "I mounted a rim above the garage this afternoon."

Basketball's the last thing I want to think about, but it's been a while since I shot hoops with Dad. I shrug. "Sure."

Mom cuts a piece off her roast beef. "I forgot to tell you, Ben. I saw your friend Ellie at lunch yesterday."

"Oh yeah?" I say, as if I don't already know about the chicken wing encounter. Buster nuzzles up against my leg, and I sneakily drop a spoonful of potatoes onto the tile for him.

Mom draws in her eyebrows. "She's such a nice girl. Why haven't I seen her or Hunter around lately?"

I know that look. She's onto me.

I shred my roast beef with my fork. "Ellie's been tutoring a lot. And Hunter has a new girlfriend." See how I manage to tell the truth even when lying? I am becoming a master falsehood-wielder indeed. A fact I'm not entirely proud of.

Abby drops her jaw dramatically like she's a character on one of those Disney Channel shows she's always watching. "Hunter has a *girlfriend*?"

Dad tsk-tsks and shakes his head. "He's too young to have a girlfriend."

"I think it's sweet," Mom says, giving me a knowing grin. "Besides, kids this age just text and invite each other to school functions. It's not like they're *really* dating."

Actually, Hunter invited Lucy to his house *and* he bought her a bagel. I don't think you can get more "really dating" than that. But I'll let her believe what she wants.

Abby swirls the potatoes around on her plate. "Don't you guys think we eat mashed potatoes a lot? There are, like, a bajillion other things we can do with the potato stash in the cupboard."

"I'd be happy to help you cook," volunteers Dad. "What should we make?"

Dad and Abby take turns suggesting future meals:

"Scalloped potatoes."

"Funeral potatoes."

"Potato soup."

"Baked potatoes."

"*Twice*-baked potatoes."

"NO . . . MORE . . . POTATOES!" I slam my fork on the table and glare at my plate. Three pairs of eyes watch me curiously, and Abby snickers under her breath.

"Are you upset about something?" Mom asks.

"Yeah." Dad sets his fork down. "Do you want to talk about it?"

I inhale through my nose. "I'm just not feeling well. I gotta go to my room."

I abandon my half-eaten food and head for the stairs.

Mom's chair squeaks back, but Dad stops her. "Just let him go, hon," he mutters. "He needs a little space."

I tromp up the stairs, Buster scrambling behind me. He's getting better at this climbing thing. Back on my bed, I curl into a semicircle around Buster, combing through his soft, sandy hair with my fingers as he rests his chin on my thigh. Something about petting dogs is therapeutic. Something about dogs in general. I rest my hand on his bony back and feel his body pulse up and down as he pants.

"Buster, Buster." I scratch him behind the ears. A low moan rumbles deep in his throat. He stands, straightening his legs.

"You okay, buddy?"

His skinny little body heaves and huffs, heaves and huffs. He opens his mouth and . . . *splat*. Dog barf. All over my jeans.

"Ewwww, Buster!" I examine the damage. Potatoes. Naturally.

After rinsing off in the bathroom and replacing my sheets, I change into my red flannel pajamas. I flick off the light and crawl under my covers, but it becomes obvious I won't be falling asleep anytime soon. Thoughts whirl around my brain like a giant tornado: *Will I survive the last game tomorrow? Will my friends hate me forever? What kind of revenge is in store for the Spud?*

I don't want to think anymore. There's only one place I can go to escape. I click on my desk lamp, prop a pillow behind my back, and open my go-to app: CloudGerbil. I rhythmically tilt my phone from side to side, helping the cartoon gerbil jump high and higher, up into the sky and away from his problems.

Somewhere around level twenty, someone taps on my door.

"Ben?" It's Mom. I lie down and slide the glowing phone under my back.

The door creaks open. "Ben," she whispers, hovering in the doorway.

I breathe deeply and pretend to be asleep, just wanting to be left alone. Miraculously, Mom sighs and shuffles her fuzzy slippers out the door.

I remain still in case this is a trap. For all I know, she'll pop back in after thirty seconds and yell, *Gotcha!* I keep my eyes shut, and soon enough, fake sleep melts into real sleep as my consciousness drifts away to join the gerbil up in the clouds.

22
Faking It

When I wake up on the day of the big game, I know I'm not getting out of bed. It's just not gonna happen.

I slap my phone off my nightstand and tap off the alarm. I nestle back into bed, but I can't get comfortable knowing Mom could pop in any second and shake me awake. I roll out of bed, clunk to the floor, and crawl to the door like a wounded zombie. I turn the lock and scurry back to bed, burying myself deep under the covers to hide from the light seeping through my windows.

At seven-forty-five a.m., Mom raps on the door. "Ben, you're gonna be late for school if you don't leave right now!" I burrow deeper into bed.

Mom starts to sing the awful wake-up song she invented when we were little. "It's a brand-new day, hey! It's a brand-new day, hey!"

I groan. "Ugh! Make it stop!"

She wiggles the locked door handle. "Benjamin, let me in."

"I'm sick," I yell from under the covers.

"Don't make me get the key."

I groan louder, wishing curses upon whoever invented the stupid master key. "Fine. Gimme a second."

I rub my palm against my forehead to heat it up. My fake sickness will be more convincing if I have a fever. Too bad I don't have a hot-water bottle or something I could hold up to my head. It'd be much more efficient.

There *is* my nightstand lamp. I left it on all night.

I flick off the lamp switch and tap the bulb with my finger. Too hot. Is this situation worth risking a third-degree burn over?

Mom pounds once. "I have to get to an appointment." She pounds twice. "That's it. I'm getting the key."

I unscrew the lamp's bulb from its socket and blow at it repeatedly like it's a trick birthday candle. I tap the bulb a few times against my forehead and wince. If this doesn't work, I'll be the world's biggest idiot.

Mom turns the handle, and I toss the light bulb under my bed. I hop onto my mattress and curl into the fetal position, trying to look as miserable as possible, which isn't too hard, given the circumstances. Mom opens the door and tromps over. She peers down at me with her hands on her hips. I squint and moan, letting my tongue hang out slightly.

She relaxes her arms. “Oh, honey, you look awful.” She feels my forehead, just as expected. “You do feel a little warm. Are you nauseous?”

“A little. Mostly weak.”

“Oh, you poor thing.” She runs her fingers through my hair. “Have you felt like this since last night? Okay, I’m going to reschedule Buster’s appointment right now. He had his follow-up with the vet today, but—”

“No, really. I’m fine. Just go.” I can’t stop Buster from going to the vet because of me. What if his worm medicine isn’t working?

Mom purses her lips. “I can’t leave you alone.”

“Mom, it’s fine. Honestly. Go to the vet.” I plead with her with my eyes. “I’ll just keep resting till you get back.”

She clicks her tongue, and worry lines appear between her brows. “Are you sure you’ll be okay for a couple of hours?”

“Mom, I’m twelve. I can handle a little fever. I just need to rest.”

She tilts her head right and left as she weighs the options and then gives in. “All right. I’ll bring you a glass of orange juice.”

She returns with a gigantic cup of orange juice—literally the largest cup we own—and watches to make sure I gulp down every last drop. Then I actually do start to feel nauseous. I don't love orange juice to begin with, but even worse, it's the kind with the pulp. Textured liquid should not exist, period. Even the sound of the word is gross. *Pulp.*

Once Mom leaves, I fidget with my Rubik's Cube and scrape the orange residue off my tongue with my teeth since I'm too lazy to grab my toothbrush. My stomach feels full and jiggly, but overall, chugging orange juice is better than facing school and whatever Duke has planned for me. Coach can't blame me for missing the last game if I'm home sick. Why didn't I think of this excuse before?

After solving the Rubik's Cube three times, I start to get bored. I scroll through my Instagram feed, and before I know it, I'm stalking Ellie's photos like a class-A creeper. She doesn't post a lot; she has maybe twelve pictures total. The latest was taken three weeks ago. She wears a white hat she crocheted herself and carries Bella, her fluffy Maltese poodle. We used to joke that we should get our dogs to breed because they'd make the cutest little corgipoos.

After that is a photo of me and Hunter wearing weird sunglasses we found at the dollar store. We look so happy.

A weird pressure starts building in my chest, like a scream is trying to escape, but I shove it back down. I go back to my feed and keep scrolling. Mindlessly scrolling. It numbs the pressure, if only just a little.

Then I come to an image that makes me stop.

It's Mitch in a field. The one right behind Sammy's Diner. It's bright and sunny and covered with snow. And hovering above his head is a neon-green quadcopter.

Mitch finally got it.

My throat starts to tingle and my nose starts to run. I can't believe I'm being so sappy about this, but something about that quadcopter makes me want to cry. Maybe it's because I'm happy for Mitch. He wanted that quadcopter, and he worked hard to get it. He's not a quitter. Not like me.

Wait. What is he wearing?

I zoom in with my thumbs and squint. A cartoon potato flexes on his chest. The game-day shirt.

I feel like a basketball has hit me in the gut. Even Mitch, who up until last week never went to the basketball games, ended up getting the shirt—and I still haven't. I promised Ellie I'd buy it, and I never did. I'm not just a quitter. I'm a bad friend.

What do I want most in the world right now? I want

my friends to trust me again. And what am I doing to gain their trust? Faking sick.

The bravest thing I've done today is chug a glass of pulpy orange juice.

I put the phone down. If I'm honest with myself, I know playing hooky isn't the answer to my problems. It won't make me happy, and it won't win me back my friends. It might get Duke and Paris off my back. But is that worth it? I'd rather be known as the dorkiest mascot alive than go through middle school without my best friends.

And I really should keep my promise to Coach. The team needs me to build their momentum. I've done it before, and I can do it again. I can help us win.

No more sitting here like a lump and pretending to be sick. No more hiding from my problems and hoping they disappear. The only person who can fix this mess is me. And it starts with getting my friends back on my side.

Turns out, some things are more important than being cool.

I text Mom: Feeling better. Heading to school.

Let's do this thing.

• • •

I pace the hall outside Ellie's fifth-period class, tapping my fingers on my thighs as I wait for the bell. I have a simple three-step plan:

1. Walk up to her.
2. Look her square in the eye.
3. Say, "I'm sorry. I'm an idiot. Can I please explain everything?"

There's no way I can mess this up.

The bell rings, and students spill out the door. When Ellie walks out, I:

1. Walk up to her.
2. Look her square in the eye—

And *she* says, "I'm sorry."

"*You're* sorry?" I sputter.

Her words come out fast. "I feel bad about chewing you out yesterday. I should have at least let you explain. I thought about this a lot, and, you know, if you don't want to eat with us, that's fine—"

"Ellie—"

"I mean, you don't have to have just one group of friends. You can take turns, like—"

I speak louder. "Ellie."

She looks at me.

"*I'm* the one who's sorry. And I do

want to eat lunch with you. This whole thing, I can explain it all. But first . . ." I pull off my hoodie to reveal what's underneath—the game-day shirt. I passed by the office to buy it ten minutes ago. Better late than never.

"Sorry it took so long for me to get this," I say. "I've been a terrible friend."

Ellie tugs on her braid and smiles a little. "At least you admit it. The shirt looks good on you, though. Where's your next class?"

I point down the hall. "That way. Why?"

"I have to go to math—that way." She points in the opposite direction. "But let's talk more at the basketball game tonight. Wanna go?" She starts walking backward. "It's at six. Hunter was gonna come, but now he's ditching me to hang out with Lucy."

I scratch the back of my neck. "Um . . ." The corners of her smile droop a little. She's probably thinking, *Oh great. All that making up and he still doesn't want to hang out with me.*

There's no time to explain. I can't just say, *Oh well, no, I can't go, but beforeyougolistenit's becauseI'mthemascot.*

So instead I say, "Yeah, sure."

"Sweet!" Ellie says. "I'm tutoring after school, so I'll just meet you in the bleachers." She whirls around and whisks down the hall.

How am I supposed to watch the game with Ellie *and* be on the court as a mascot?

I'm doomed.

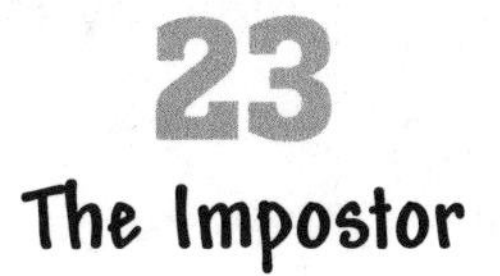

23
The Impostor

I stroll into the gym ten minutes early, wearing my game-day shirt and brown leggings under my jeans. My plan is basic: I'll tell Ellie why I can't sit with her and then rush to change into the Spud suit. I couldn't find her after school, so I only have a few minutes to catch her before the game starts.

I've never seen the gym so packed before. Up in the bleachers, fans cram shoulder to shoulder like crayons in a box. On the court, the teams are warming up. Our opponents wear blue jerseys that say TEAM TORNADO. What's their mascot, anyway? Some kid wound up in black string?

I scan the stands for Ellie, and it feels like I'm playing Where's Waldo because almost everyone's wearing red.

Finally I spot her sitting in the center section behind the band. She's taken her braid out, so her hair falls down in loose waves.

I pull up my hood to hide my face from Coach and head her way. Someone else catches me, though.

"Ben!" Mitch leaves his spot on the first row of bleachers and jogs up to me. "What are you doing?" he whispers. "Why aren't you in the suit?"

"Sorry, Mitch, no time to talk. I have to get to Ellie."

He looks confused. "You're ditching being the Spud, then?"

"No. It's complicated. She doesn't know I'm the mascot. Look, I'll have to explain later." I shrug at Mitch and jog up the rattly bleachers. I side-shuffle past a few eighth graders to get to Ellie.

"Hey!" I stretch out my arm to give her a side hug—the only type of hug that's possible in such a crowded situation.

She yells into my ear. "Finally, we get to watch a game together."

"Yeah." Except not. *Not once I tell you the truth.*

The band stops playing, so I take advantage of the relative quietness. "Ellie," I begin.

"Yeah?" She looks at me, and I notice the cool golden rings around her pupils.

I inhale. "I have to go."

She cranes her neck. "What? Why?"

Coach Tudy's head glistens with sweat as he stares at the double doors, waiting for me. It's getting late.

I lean in close so my mouth is just an inch from Ellie's ear. "I'm the—"

Waaaah, waaaah, waaaaah, waaah, wamp-wamp! yells the tuba, and the band busts out a brassy rendition of "We Will Rock You." I jolt with surprise, my lips brushing the tip of Ellie's ear. She hunches her shoulders and laughs. "Um. What are you doing?"

"Sorry!" I shout over the instruments. My ears feel like they just came out of the toaster. "I was just trying to tell you something!"

"Huh?" she yells.

It's too loud for her to hear. Holy guacamole, fate is *not* making it easy for me to come clean. Maybe it's a sign I should just keep my mouth shut.

Coach's voice echoes in my head: *If you set your mind on something, nothing will get in your way.* I can do this. I just have to get creative. I pull out my phone and draft a note: I'm the mascot. I hold the phone in front of Ellie's face and brace myself for the reaction.

Ellie stares at the screen, her eyes doubling in size as the realization sinks in. Then she snaps her head toward me. Scrunched-up eyebrows. Wide-open mouth. She's definitely angry.

It's a good thing I'm out of time, because all I want to do is run away. I can't bear to see her look at me like that anymore. "I'm sorry!" I yell as I shuffle toward the steps. "I have to go."

I clank down the steps and out the gym door. I dash for the closet, glancing behind me to make sure no one's around. As much as it stank to tell Ellie the truth, at least now it's over. It feels like I took off a backpack full of rocks.

Now that she knows who I am, I have to show her the best performance of my life. It's my very last game, so I might as well go all out. Plus, if I get the fans pumped enough, I might avoid the revenge plot. No one wants to mess with a potato if he's got the crowd on his side.

In the closet, I jump into the suit, plunk on the head-piece, click the latches, and slam the door shut on my way out. I've never changed so fast in my life—and that's saying something coming from a guy who's running late ninety percent of the time.

As I walk over to the bench, a few kids heckle me from behind.

"Hey, Mr. Potato Head, get off our team!"

"Hey, loser! You're a loser!"

So clever. I let their words bounce right off my foam costume like hot dogs bouncing off a wall. I'm a tough potato. One with thick skin.

I twirl like a ballerina, prance over to where the loudest heckler is sitting, and blow a kiss right in his face. The people around him laugh. That shuts him up him pretty good.

Down on the court, the game is about to start. Duke and a Tornadoes player stride to the center line and glare at each other like archnemeses. A lot hinges on this game. Whichever team wins will be sent to the playoffs. Whichever loses is done until next year.

The official tosses the ball into the air, and Duke tips it to Seth. Seth catches the ball and chest-passes it back to Duke, who dribbles it all the way downcourt and makes a layup. The crowd erupts with cheers. Ten seconds in, and we're off to a good start.

I hop down the sidelines, pumping my arms with all the energy of a toddler hyped up on sugar. Then I pace the bleachers to find fans who are sitting and help them to their feet. I'm Steve the Spud: King of Momentum. No one sits on my watch!

After several minutes, Coach flashes a hand signal at

the ref, who blows the whistle for a time-out. I step onto the court and begin an energetic cha-cha slide.

"Hey, Spudboy! Get off the stage!" yells one of the hecklers from before.

"Yeah," says his friend. "Your dancing stinks!"

You can't win 'em all. But I really don't care. I cup my hand to my ear to show I won't let them get to me. Then, just to annoy them, I pull out a series of the cheesiest dance moves in American history: I walk like an Egyptian. I frame my face. I do the Shopping Cart, the Sprinkler, and, of course, the Mashed Potato. I peek at Ellie up in the stands. She's shaking her head and cracking up. She definitely wouldn't be laughing like that if she hated me. Maybe she'll forgive me after all.

A bolt of energy runs through me, and like an impulse, I throw my hands on the floor and kick my feet up in the air. I channel my energy to balance on my hands, tightening my ab muscles to keep from wobbling. After three seconds or so, I come back down and take a bow to whistles and stomps. I didn't think it was possible. A potato handstand! Nothing can stop me now.

At halftime, we're up by twelve. So far, so good: no revenge plot in sight. I think I can manage to slip back into the stands to sit by Ellie for a bit. Coach said student council is taking over for halftime, so I'm not really needed. Halftime lasts about fifteen minutes, so that's plenty of time to get up there and beg Ellie for forgiveness.

The cheerleaders start their routine, and I disappear into the hall. I run to the closet and heave my round self through the doorway like a whale through a hoop. I throw on my clothes with supersonic speed and slip back into the gym with my hands in my pockets like nothing ever happened. I've got a knack for this double-agent stuff.

I catch Ellie's eye, and her face practically explodes into a smile. I quicken my pace.

I'M A JIGGLY JELL-O MAN
YOU'RE A JIGGLY JELL-O FAN
JIGGLY JIGGLY JELL-O IN YOUR TUM

The annoying commercial jingle blares from my pocket, and a few people shoot me funny looks. I can't believe I forgot to change that stupid text-message alert. Whoever it is will have to wait.

As I jog up the bleachers, I scan the sidelines for Coach. What would he say if he saw me up here? Luckily, he's leading the team to the locker room, so he'll never know I disappeared. I reach Ellie's row and side-shuffle my way past the same eighth graders as before.

"Why'd you come back?" Ellie asks.

"I have a little time," I say. "I wanted to sit with you, like we planned."

"Well, good." She crosses her arms. "Because I have a *lot* of questions."

"I'll start from the beginning." I lean in and talk just loud enough so that only she can hear. "Remember two weeks ago when I threw that hot dog in the cafeteria? Remember how I—"

I choke on a gasp and splutter to a stop.

"Ben, are you okay? What's wrong?" Ellie demands.

But I can't speak, because a round figure is looming in the doorway.

And into the gymnasium walks Steve the Spud.

24
Revenge Is a Dish Best Served Mashed

The Spud walks to the bench and wobbles as he sits. I gape at him from the bleachers, feeling like I'm going through one of those out-of-body experiences.

"You look like you've seen a ghost," Ellie says.

I blink hard, hoping she's right. Nope, he's real. Definitely real. "Uh, Ellie," I say. "Did you see anyone leave the gym while I was gone?"

"Did I see anyone leave the gym?" she repeats like it's the most ridiculous question in the world.

I point at the Spud.

She makes a face. "Who's that?"

"I wish I knew."

I mentally replay everything that happened since my court appearance. I slipped out of the gym, into the closet, out of the suit, into the hall, and back into the gym. A lot of slipping occurred, and it was all very sneaky. No one was watching me in the halls—I'm sure of it.

But in my rush to get back to the stands, I probably forgot to lock the closet door behind me. Someone *could* have slunk into the closet after I left and hijacked the suit. I run through some possible suspects:

1. Paris. Maybe she's planning on committing a crime and framing me.

2. Wyatt. Maybe he's fully recovered and found himself unable to resist returning to his beloved suit.

3. The suit itself. Maybe it's under a curse and came to life. I always knew something was creepy about it.

"Is that your phone?" Ellie asks.

The question crashes my train of thought. "Huh?"

"Your pocket," Ellie says. "It beeped."

I pull my phone out and slide my thumb across the screen. The beep was notifying me of the unopened message from three minutes ago.

It's from Mitch: I see what you're doing, trying to be in two places at once. Ellie's gonna catch on if you keep switching in and out of the suit. I'll take over from here. Enjoy the game 😊

I shove my phone into my pocket.

"Who was it?" asks Ellie.

"Mitch." I clamp my tongue between my teeth. He must have misunderstood me when I saw him before the game. He thinks I'm tricking Ellie, and he's trying to cover for me.

As the cheerleaders finish up their halftime routine, Mitch stands on top of the wooden bench and does the Twist, only to be met with boos from the same annoying hecklers as before. This isn't right. This is my battle to fight, not his. I have to get down there and convince him to switch back with me ASAP.

"So, are you and Mitch *both* the Spud?" Ellie asks, confused.

There's not enough time in the world for all the things I'll have to explain when this is over.

"No. Just me. I hate to run off again, but I've got to get down there. I'll see you after the game."

"Okay?" Ellie says. She's probably so sick of all this nonsense. I didn't even have time to apologize. I'm really pushing my luck.

As I jog down the bleachers, Paris speaks into a microphone from center court. "How you doing, Spuds?" The crowd cheers in response. Beside her, some of the other student-council kids spread a giant plastic tarp over one side of the court.

"Thank you all for coming out to cheer on our awesome team!" Paris says when the applause dies down. "Student council has arranged a very special show for you tonight. Bring it on out, guys!"

I reach the bottom of the bleachers and squeeze myself onto the end of the front row. Mitch sits on his bench ten feet in front of me and to the side. "Mitch," I whisper forcefully, planning to motion him out the door when he turns around.

Mitch watches the court as the same five kids who laid down the plastic tarp drag a large blow-up kiddie pool out from under the guest bleachers. I crane my neck to see what's inside, but with no luck.

"Mitch," I whisper with more urgency. Who am I kidding? A whisper can't penetrate that foam headpiece. I'll have to wait until he turns around. I want to just go tug on his arm, but it would be way too embarrassing to walk out in front of everyone.

I forget my mission for a moment as the student-council members drag the kiddie pool to the middle of the tarp. What's in there anyway? It looks . . . white?

"Here we have a pool full of mashed potatoes!" Paris announces with a flourish of her hand. The audience oohs and aahs. Everyone stretches their necks to get a better view. The blue inflatable pool is about four feet in diameter and two feet deep with runny potato goop. Someone must have dumped like a hundred boxes of instant potatoes in there.

Paris points at the pool. "Hidden inside is a golf ball. We'll call three volunteers from the audience, and whoever finds it wins a fifty-dollar gift card to Sammy's Diner!"

The noise level is out of control. Students, siblings, and even a few parents wave their hands wildly in the air.

Ooooh, pick me! the impulsive part of my brain begs. I could use fifty bucks' worth of ice cream! My hand shoots up to volunteer, but then I remember I have a more meaningful task at hand.

I lower my hand. "Mitch," I call louder. Again, he doesn't budge.

Paris selects the first two volunteers, and they trot down the stands. "I need one more volunteer," she says. "Raise those hands high!"

I pan the crowd. Everyone's distracted enough for me to pull Mitch out of the gym without making a scene. Paris picks the third volunteer—Coach's nephew, the Lost Boy look-alike who chased me after the last game. He does a goofy victory dance before running to the court.

Just then, Duke and Cole appear in the doorway. Aren't they supposed to be in the locker room?

They crouch low and run up behind Mitch's bench. Duke grabs the foam head with his beefy hands and yanks. The headpiece slips off as easily as a pen cap, since Mitch didn't attach the latches.

"No!" I stand. Those jerks!

Duke tosses the head onto the court and, with Cole's help, swiftly hoists Mitch into the air. The boys spin Mitch toward the stands to expose his pale, openmouthed face.

Gasps erupt from my section. "Hey, it's that one kid!" one of the hecklers says.

A tornado of anger whirls in my chest. "Cut it out!"

Duke doesn't hear me. "Dunk the Spud!" he roars.

The audience rips their attention from Paris and her volunteers to Duke and Cole. They haul Mitch across the court, lugging him sideways like a giant cannon. I can't let them get away with this.

I charge for the microphone, my feet pounding against the court. I've never run faster in my entire life. Not even when I was being chased by the rabid fans.

"What's going on?" Paris says into the microphone, all high-pitched and innocent. She doesn't fool me. This little stunt has her name written all over it.

I yank the microphone out of Paris's hand and yell, "STOP!"

The crowd falls dead silent. Duke freezes, confusion spreading across his face as he drops his end of the potato suit. The weight of everyone's attention presses down on me. I'm center stage, all eyes on me, and I've forgotten my lines.

Just then, Coach appears in the doorway, and we make eye contact. He lifts his chin and folds his arms. I can almost hear him telepathically communicate: *Finish this, Hardy.*

"He's not really the Spud!" My voice echoes across the gym. "I am!"

The crowd starts to murmur.

"That's right." I gasp for air. "Mitch is just trying to sub for me, so leave him alone! He's the coolest guy here, and a great friend. *I* tripped Duke. And *I* knocked down the cheerleaders." The crowd's clamor grows to an all-time high. "And *I* did the cool skateboarding tricks," I quickly add.

Duke smiles devilishly and gives Cole what I can only interpret as a *let's get him* nod. I have no choice. I can either be tossed in the pool against my will, or—

"CANNONBALL!" I drop the mic with a clang and run

full speed to the potato pool. I leap into the air and land inside with a smack, potatoes splattering over the inflatable sides.

The potato goop seeps into my mouth and ears. I can't believe I just did that. I'm getting so busted.

The ref blows his whistle like crazy, but I'm not done yet. I have to show Duke that that was the *last* time he'll mess with me and Mitch. I emerge from the pool a giant potato monster, globs of goo dripping off my body. I scoop up a handful and chuck it at Duke. The potato snowball falls apart on its way through the air and splatters across his jersey. Perfect shot.

Duke's face hardens and he lunges for me. I jump to the side, but my shoes slip on the plastic tarp. I slide straight into Paris, who topples into a volunteer and falls on her butt. Again.

"Agghhh!" she cries, smacking potatoes off her legs like they're mosquitoes.

"Food fight!" The Lost Boy gallops toward the pool. The other volunteers exchange a glance and run to the pool as well. They probably still believe there's a golf ball in there.

About half a dozen kids, including Wyatt and the pit-bull boy, rush down from the bleachers to join. Coach and the ref run around trying to shoo everyone away, but to no avail. They would be better off shooing a drove of bees from a hive.

More kids spill onto the court, probably thinking they can't get in trouble when they're part of such a large group. The student announcer cranks the music over the speakers and abandons his corner table. Even a couple of cheerleaders venture onto the court. Not Jayla, though. She and most of the squad desert their courtside spot to seek shelter in the top rows of the bleachers.

Pretty soon the court is full of kids flinging potato

goop at each other. Duke's so caught up in the food fight he seems to have forgotten he was chasing me. "This is awesome!" he yells as he slops a handful onto the back of Paris's neck.

"Blagh." Her fingers curl into fists.

Mitch lies on his back in the middle of the madness, squirming like a worm. I tug down on the suit so he can wiggle out of the top.

He kicks the empty suit like it deserves a punishment. "Thanks, dude."

"Anytime," I say. "Thanks for trying to cover for me."

A couple of parents join Coach and the ref, but by now it's them against twenty, a lost cause. Students dart around the adults, avoiding them like they're playing tag. Once the pool is empty, they resort to scooping spuds off the floor and reflinging them. The Lost Boy is the most boisterous of all. He takes off his shirt and smacks anyone in his path, laughing like a maniac. Others roll around the tarp like pigs in mud so they can go hug someone who's clean.

I've just scooped some potatoes off the tarp, preparing to nail Mitch, when someone grabs my shoulder and whirls me around.

Ellie's eyes pierce into me. Her shirt's a little speckled, but for the most part, she's clean.

"What were you thinking?" she yells. "Why didn't you tell me?"

I let the potatoes in my hand fall to the court. "You must think I'm such an idiot."

"Obviously," she says, but a smile touches the corners of her lips. Suddenly I'm completely out of breath, and I don't think it's because of the potato fight.

I step forward. "Ellie, I'm sorry. For everything. I lied to you. I was so embarrassed. I thought if I could get through these past two weeks, no one would ever have to know. But there's no excuse. I really blew it. I—"

Before I can finish, she leans forward and kisses me. Right on the lips. I freeze like a stun gun shot me in the face.

"Ben," she says. "You didn't blow it. Or, if you did, this is the most epic fail ever."

I look around and realize she's right. Mitch is chasing Cole and looking happier than I've ever seen. Paris is filling a shoe full of potatoes, probably meant for Duke. Wyatt has stolen the Lost Boy's shirt and is smacking him back in retaliation. This is the coolest halftime show ever.

And Ellie. She just kissed me. It doesn't get any better than that. I put my hand on her shoulder and take in her smile and her dimples and her beautiful hair, which I'll definitely be able to brush out of her eyes from now on. I close my eyes and lean in for another kiss.

Smat. She slaps potatoes in my face and runs off laughing.

I gasp and wipe away the salty goop. "You asked for it, Ellie!" I scoop some potatoes off the court, and the chase is on.

Overall, that was *not* how I imagined my first kiss would go.

I never could've thought up something so awesome.

25
The Aftermath

It's been two weeks since the Mashed Potato Incident, and I'm still dealing with the aftermath. I've developed a rare form of PTSD called post-traumatic spud disorder, where every time I see a potato, my hands start to feel clammy and my knees start to shake and my fingers reach for my ears to make sure no potatoes are still in there.

Okay, okay, it's not that dramatic, but I have fun playing it up. Like, whenever I see potatoes, I pretend to faint and fall on the floor. I straight up told my mom I'd have to stop eating her mashed potatoes for a while, and surprisingly, she obliged. Dad must have been grateful I got her to stop making the potato glue, because he bought us tickets for a Utah Jazz game next month, and we're gonna take a mini road trip. Their mascot is the firework-spewing motorcycle bear from YouTube, and I can't wait to see him in person. Who knew I'd become such a mascot fanboy?

The food fight on the court didn't last much longer. After a minute of chasing Ellie, I noticed Coach Tudy, the ref, and the parent helpers really starting to look worn out. I grabbed the mic and told everyone we should get off the court—that the potatoes were drying out anyway. Surprisingly, they listened.

Everyone who'd participated in the food fight was kicked out of the gym. (Everyone they could catch, anyway.) Coach shook his head at me as I walked past him. "Look at the disaster you've caused, Hardy. You should've stepped off the stage after your speech. Quit while you were ahead."

"I'm sorry, Coach," I said. "But winners never quit, you know?"

"You're no quitter, I'll give you that." He pointed me out the door. "But don't expect to avoid the consequences."

Mitch texted us the game results when it was over. Apparently, Coach made Duke and Cole sit out the whole second half, but we didn't need them anyway. The Mashed Potato Incident had garnered so much momentum that our crowd cheered our team on to victory. Mitch said Coach was jumping all over the place like a little kid, ecstatic that we made the playoffs.

That night I told my mom and dad everything that had happened at the game (except for Ellie's kiss, obviously). I figured the school would call them anyway, so I'd rather they heard it from me first. Plus, whenever you fess up to something, parents are a lot more compassionate.

They grounded me for two weeks, which is the same I got for reading books during math in fifth grade, so it could've been worse. Mom said I deserved a month, but since I'd effectively grounded myself during the two weeks when I was the mascot, she let me count that toward my punishment.

The Monday after the food fight, I got called into Principal Jensen's office during second period.

"You know, Ben, I like you," he said once I'd made myself comfortable in the leather swivel chair in front of his desk. "I think you're a good kid. In fact, you remind me a lot of myself when I was your age. 'Pleasantly disruptive,' my teachers called it." He chuckled.

Principal Jensen cleared his throat. "Now, what you did on Friday, I heard it was quite the show. But, unfortunately, there have to be some consequences for your actions."

Here comes the suspension, I thought. *Bring it on.*

"We're going to have to suspend you for two days."

Whoomp, there it is.

"We try to avoid out-of-school suspensions if possible, but this is what our administration has concluded. We've received numerous parental complaints. It really tainted our school's reputation. And you know how we feel about food-throwing." He shrugged as if to say, *What can ya do?* "Now, generally, suspension means you cannot participate in any school-related activities for the rest of the quarter. *However,* Coach Tudy informed me that your mascot performance played a big factor in our team's historic win. So you may resume attending school-related events beginning February twenty-first."

I counted the days in my head. "That's the day of the dance."

"Is it?" He winked. "I had no idea. Oh, and one more thing."

Gulp.

"You can't run for student council or be elected head of any clubs. It's too bad, really. I think you have great leadership potential."

Only a guy like Principal Jensen can call you to his office to punish you, yet leave you feeling better about yourself. "Ms. Wu said the same thing. I never considered myself a leader, but I guess I've changed a lot since moving here."

He nodded thoughtfully. "Well, maybe you can run a club next year. Or even start one."

"Yeah, maybe."

And I meant it. I've been thinking we need a spirit club, like a group that promotes school pride and makes posters and stuff. We could even run a fund-raiser to order a new mascot suit. That thing reeks, especially now that it's all crusty with dried potatoes.

I've been looking for a replacement suit online, but they're running upward of three hundred bucks. Who knew a brown sack of foam could be so expensive?

News of the food fight spread like wildfire. After I got back from the principal's office, everyone was asking me about what happened.

At lunch, Duke came over to my table to talk about our punishments from the principal. He said it was all worth it—that we put on "the sickest halftime show in South Fork history." Ha! It's like he thought we planned the whole thing together. Apparently he forgot how much he used to hate me for tripping him with the potato. That guy has either a super-forgiving heart or a super-bad memory.

Duke said he, Paris, and Cole got suspensions too. Paris tried to plead innocent, but Duke outed her as the mastermind behind the whole operation. They broke up, which lasted for a record forty-eight hours before they were back together again. In addition to their suspensions, the three received a weeklong sentence of peeling potatoes for the cafeteria. As bad as that sounds, word is that Paris is more upset she can't run for student council again. Personally, I think we're much better off without someone like her in power.

Tonight, my grounding sentence is finally over—just in time for the dance. I'm meeting up with Hunter, Ellie, and Mitch. It's funny how we all wound up dateless. Ellie canceled on Cole. She wasn't impressed with his dunk-the-Spud routine. Hunter found out Lucy hated peanut butter and was so appalled that he told her he'd rather just be friends. And Jayla has wanted nothing to do with me since finding out I was the Spud, which I guess I deserve. I really didn't treat her the way I should have. I texted her an apology after the game, and she responded with: Just so you know, I'll go out with you again when pigs fly. This time there were no pink balloons.

I dig my South Fork Spuds game-day shirt out of my dresser and pull it over my head. Ellie will get a kick out of it. Besides, the muscly potato dude is growing on me.

Mom knocks on the door. "Can I come in?"

"Yeah."

Mom enters and looks me up and down. "Isn't this a formal dance?"

"Semiformal." I point to my slacks. "Half formal." I point to my shirt. "Half not."

She sighs. "You know that's not what 'semiformal' means, right?"

"Yeah." I put on my shoes. "It's like an inside joke with Ellie."

"Speaking of Ellie . . ." Mom pulls a wrist corsage from behind her back. "I thought she would love this." She grins down at the flower bracelet. There are four mini pink rosebuds surrounded by those white ball-looking things. Angel's breath? Baby's breath? Someone's breath.

I shake my head. "A corsage? No way. That's so over the top. We're going with a group."

Mom tries to put it in my hand. "Oh, come on, she's going to love it! Just give it to her. Please."

"Fine," I grumble. This will be so embarrassing. Maybe I'll hide it behind my back and chuck it in the trash before anyone sees.

Mom cheers softly to herself. "Are you ready to go?"

I look over the corsage. Actually, I might be able to make this work. "Give me a second."

I go downstairs to the kitchen windowsill and pluck a leaf off Mom's new basil plant. I tear the leaf into pieces and shove them in between the roses of the corsage. Ellie's going to love it.

Mom walks up behind me. She grimaces at my creation and tries to sound encouraging. "That's lovely."

Five minutes later, Mom drops me off in front of the gym. I walk inside and breathe in the warm air. The gym looks so different all dressed up. White, twinkly lights hang from the ceiling. Tables are grouped into one corner, decorated with blue tablecloths and paper snowflakes. Silver balloons are tethered to the tables, and six giant foam snowmen stand around the sidelines, doubling as backup chaperones.

Coach stands in one corner of the gym looking pretty fancy with his dark jeans and a black button-down shirt. I've only ever seen him in T-shirts before. He folds his arms and taps his feet to the music.

I join Ellie and Hunter at one of the tables. Ellie has on black leggings and a flowy red dress. Of course she's wearing South Fork colors. But for once, I get to one-up her in the school-spirit category.

I take off my jacket and set it in my lap. Ellie does a double take at my game-day shirt and beams at me. I have to admit, I finally have Spud pride.

Hunter smirks a little when I slip the corsage onto Ellie's wrist, but at least she appreciates it. She keeps sniffing it and telling me how good it smells and how I definitely have a future in corsage design.

"So, how does it feel to finally be ungrounded?" Hunter asks, twirling one of the paper snowflakes around his finger.

"Amazing," I say. "I hate being stuck in my room."

"It's too bad you couldn't get off the hook one day early," Ellie says. "You would've loved the game last night. The crowd was going wild! First Spud championship win in like twenty years!"

"I wish I could've seen it." I catch Coach's eye in the corner of the gym, and we wave to each other. I wonder if he'll retire now that his team took state. I'll miss him if he does.

"It was awesome!" Hunter slams the snowflake down. "We obliterated those stupid Jackrabbits! Wyatt even bumped their mascot and made him fall down. I think he was trying to get revenge for you."

"Ha! Please tell me Mitch recorded it."

"Yep," Ellie says. "He was determined to capture everything."

"Where is he, anyway?" I ask.

As if on cue, the gym door opens and Mitch comes in with his puffy orange jacket.

"We're up to four thousand two hundred and nineteen

views!" He heads to our table, holding his phone above his head. I told him he could upload the skateboarding video to his YouTube channel, and he's been updating me on the view count like twice a day.

Mitch sits next to Hunter. "Check out some of these comments." He reads off his phone. "MASCOT-MAFIA244 says, 'Best mascot ever! This guy wins at life.'"

I scoff. "Yeah, right."

"Come on, you were a great mascot," Ellie says. "In fact, I think you should take over next year when Wyatt goes to high school."

I shake my head. "No, thank you. Never again."

She whispers in my ear. "I thought it was really cool how you came out on your skateboard." My stomach does a somersault.

"What are you saying to him?" Hunter asks. "You guys can't act gushy around me! We agreed!"

Ellie backs away a little, and I cringe at the awkwardness of Hunter's comment.

"You know," I say to everyone, "I've been thinking about my potato curse."

"Not this again." Ellie grabs some chips from the bowl on our table.

"I believe you," Mitch says. "You have some solid evidence."

"I believe you too!" Hunter says. "I mean, he broke his arm by tripping over a bag of potatoes. That doesn't just *happen*, Ellie."

"Actually," I say, "I don't think I'm cursed anymore."

Ellie looks impressed. "Is that so?"

"Yeah. I've been going over things in my mind, and I haven't suffered a single potato-related disaster since the Mashed Potato Incident."

I have yet another reason to believe the curse is broken, but I don't say it out loud since it falls into the "gushy" category. You know how in fairy tales, curses are always broken by a kiss? Well, kissing Ellie while covered in potatoes seems to have done the trick. We must have appeased the Potato God's wrath, causing the curse to lift off me and fly out the gym door.

"I don't buy it," Hunter says. "The curse is just taking a break." He bites into a potato chip and yelps, his hand shooting up to cover his mouth. "I bith mah tongue!" he says through a mouthful of chips. "Owww."

Out on the dance floor, a slow song starts to play. I don't know the title, but I know all the words because my mom always belts it out dramatically when it comes on the radio.

"Let's dance," Ellie says, pulling me out onto the floor. We pass Jayla dancing with Cole. I nod at Jayla. I'm glad she found someone else to go with. Surprisingly, she nods back.

Ellie puts her hands on my shoulders, and I completely blank on what I'm supposed to do next. I sneak a peek at some of the other dancing couples and remember I'm supposed to put my hands on her waist. I do, and start swaying back and forth.

"You're a pretty good dancer," Ellie says.

"Obviously," I say. "You saw my mascot moves. I'm a natural."

"It's true," she says. "I've never seen someone so naturally crash into a cheer pyramid."

"Not everyone's born with the gift." Just then, I step on her toes. "Oops," I say. But she doesn't seem to mind.

Over at our table, Mitch is tossing potato chips and Hunter's running around to catch them in his mouth. Mitch tosses a chip up high, and Hunter leans his head back to catch it. He runs backward, mouth open, and bumps into one of the foam snowmen. The potato chip lands in Hunter's mouth.

"Yeah! Who's good?" Hunter brags. "I never miss!"

At that moment, the snowman falls over, and its head detaches.

"Speaking of that potato curse," says Ellie, "you don't think Hunter caught it, do you?"

"Nah," I say. But then I watch as Hunter scrambles across the gym to catch the snowman's rolling head. "Actually, you might be onto something."

The song's coming to an end, so I whip out the move from one of my daydreams. I twirl Ellie three times and then lower her in a dip. I'd say my execution is a seven out of ten. At least I don't drop her.

After that, a fast song begins to play. Hunter and Mitch join us.

"Let's do all the cheesy dance moves Ben did as the mascot," Ellie says.

Mitch does the Sprinkler. "This was my favorite."

"What about this one?" Ellie walks like an Egyptian.

"My favorite was that Mashed Potato dance," Hunter says. "Didn't it go like this?"

I stop moonwalking. "Hunter, I wouldn't do that if I were—"

But it's too late. He's doing the Mashed Potato, shuffling backward as he twists his legs out from side to side. Before I know it, he rams into a parent chaperone who's carrying a giant bowl of potato chips to one of the tables.

The bowl flies into the air, and chips rain down like confetti. The metal bowl clangs and skids across the gym, chips scattering everywhere. Several people squeal and jump out of the bowl's path, and then everyone turns to stare at Hunter.

I hate to say it, but the evidence is clear.

"Hunter." I put on my most serious expression. "It appears the curse has chosen its next victim."

He tosses his head back and yells at the ceiling, "Noooooooo!"

Poor Hunter. But if I got through the curse, so will he. At least he's got me, Ellie, and Mitch to help him out.

I help Hunter to his feet. "Rule number one: Be on red alert whenever potatoes are around."

He whimpers.

"Rule number two: You can still eat fries, but chew carefully."

"Why me?"

"Rule number three: Leave the Mashed Potato dancing to me."

Then I break it down. A circle forms around me as I Mashed Potato like my life depends on it. One by one, people start to join in until eventually even Duke, Paris, Jayla, and Cole are Mashed Potatoing it up.

I look around and let the moment soak in—dorky dance moves, no more secrets, and the feeling of only wanting to be exactly where I am.

I've experienced a lot of ups and downs this past month. But the most unexpected thing of all?

This potato-obsessed town is starting to feel like home.

ACKNOWLEDGMENTS

I feel overwhelmed by the support I've received throughout this publishing process.

A huge thank-you to Amber Caravéo, my brilliant and tireless agent. After a seemingly endless string of rejections, you were my first "yes." You believed in me and my funny little story, and that completely changed my life.

To my editor, Chelsea Eberly: I am so thrilled my book found a home with you. Thank you for your kindness, helpfulness, and overall awesomeness. Your enthusiasm for this project has meant everything!

I'm beyond grateful to the whole Sales, Marketing, and Publicity team at Random House Children's Books for working to get this book into the hands of readers. To the talented designer, Bob Bianchini; the amazing cover and interior artist, James Lancett; my brilliant copyeditors, Karen Sherman and Barbara Bakowski; and wonderful production manager, Shameiza Ally. Thanks also to Kelly Delaney for the early love.

I was blessed to be chosen for Pitch Wars in 2017. Shari Schwarz, my mentor, worked tirelessly with me on this manuscript, and I'm so lucky to have her as a friend.

The Pitch Wars class of 2017 has been the best support system. I've loved chatting, venting, and celebrating together. Particular thanks to Colleen Bennett and Shelly Steig for being my best buds. You both are hilarious, and the world needs your words.

Where would I be without my family? Mom, you read through this manuscript after every major revision—and there were a lot! I'm grateful for your feedback and faith. You always believed I could do anything I set my mind to, and it started to rub off on me. Dad, you've always been my most vocal cheerleader, and I appreciate your support. Kevin, the sweetest of husbands, without you, I don't know if I could have worked my way out of all those plot holes. Thank you for your stubborn insistence that I would get published, despite my focus on the seemingly impossible odds. You are my better two-thirds, and I love you.

I cherish the members of our short-lived but very fun Ridgecrest writers group: Ronelle, Christina, Beth, Anne, Holly, Kelsey, and especially Amy. (Without your encouragement, I never would have entered Pitch Wars and might never have learned how to properly revise. I miss talking about writing with you.)

This book would not have turned out how it did without the generous feedback I received from dozens of friends. There are more of you than I can even name, but please know that your opinions were invaluable. I'm especially grateful to those who read the whole manuscript, even in its ugly early stages: Kristen Cook, Lizzie and Scott McClellan, Molly Zucknick, Sarah Kapit, Peggy Sheridan, Cori Vella, Karah Sutton, my sisters Alysha and Makynzi, Colleen, and Shelly. And special thanks to Derek Hale for reading the manuscript to his students. They drew some of the coolest book covers!

To all my seventh graders from Payson Junior High, I originally wrote this book with you in mind. You were fun and spirited and full of light, and you inspired this book more than you realize.

I can't forget all my past English teachers for helping me develop a passion for reading and writing.

Finally, I could not accomplish anything without God, who gives me inspiration, direction, and the strength to persevere past self-doubt. I aim to always use my talents in ways that are pleasing to Him.

ABOUT THE AUTHOR

ARIANNE COSTNER is a former English teacher who firmly believes that writers should crack up at their own jokes. Born and raised in Mesa, Arizona, as the oldest of five, she lives outside Los Angeles with her husband and children. Her favorite kind of potato is Tater Tots, with mashed potatoes coming in a close second—as long as they're not gluey.

ariannecostner.com